Power Ballads

The

Iowa

Short

Fiction

Award

In honor of James O. Freedman

University of

Iowa Press

Iowa City

Will Boast

Power
Ballads

University of Iowa Press, Iowa City 52242
www.uiowapress.org

Printed in the United States of America
The University of Iowa Press is a member of Green Press
Initiative and is committed to preserving natural resources.
Printed on acid-free paper

ISBN-13: 978-1-60938-042-7

ISBN-10: 1-60938-042-8

LCCN: 2011924839

For AJB, NPB, RJB

Contents

ACKNOWLEDGMENTS

These stories first appeared in the following publications: "Beginners," *American Scholar;* "Coda," *Narrative;* "Mr. Fern, Freestyle," *Five Points;* "Sidemen," *FiveChapters;* "Lost Coast," *ZYZZYVA;* and "The Bridge" (as "Diplomats"), *Glimmer Train.*

Thanks to Alyce Miller, Ann Beattie, Caitlin Satchell, Cal Morgan, Carol Edgarian, Chris Tilghman, Dave Daley, Deborah Eisenberg, Drew Johnson, Eleanor Henderson, Elizabeth Tallent, Erin Brown, Gina Welch, Halsted St, Jason Labbe, John Casey, John L'Heureux, Kim Philley, Linda Swanson-Davies, Mary Austin Speaker, Robert Wilson, Robin Metz, Samrat Upadhyay, Skip Horack, Sudip Bose, Susan Burmeister-Brown, the Sovereign Nation, Stanford University, Tobias Wolff, Tom Franklin, Tom Jenks, the Truman Capote Literary Trust, Tuesday nights at the Red Line Tap, and the University of Virginia.

To friends and family, though I can't thank you enough, all my gratitude. And all my love.

*Power
Ballads*

Sitting In

I remember all those great bands. Those bands that played pizza joints, VFW halls, and schnitzel houses all over southeast Wisconsin. Don Gruetzmacher's Green Notes, the Tom Dombrowski Seven, Die Musikmeisters, Jan Debaum and His Polka Bums, the Swingin' Udders. My mother had died a couple years back, and Dad still didn't know what to do with me. I'd just started playing tuba in the school wind ensemble (the director insisted I had a tubist's lips—I took him at his word), and Dad indulged my new mania, sometimes driving us as far as Sheboygan to see a group I'd read about in the paper. Pretty soon I was sitting in with every band I could. There didn't seem to be a leader out there able to resist seeing a skinny twelve-year-old kid, his rosy cheeks puffed out, blatting away on "Roll Out the Barrel."

But then Dad tired of ferrying me all around the tricounty area, and we settled for Sunday nights at Wenzel's, the little tavern in town where Bob "Buck" Schlachtenhaufen and the Thirty-Pointers played from seven at night till one in the morning. Buck played a huge red-leather and mother-of-pearl accordion and emceed the evening, welcoming everyone in his thickly accented English, sometimes slipping into German when he addressed certain of the musicians. The crowd was nearly all first- and second-generation Germans, Czechs, and Poles, with a few old-timers who'd come straight off the boat, so to speak.

"So this is where they all hang out," Dad said the first time we went to Wenzel's. "Christ, they keep to themselves, don't they? They ought to mix more, you know, be part of the community." He was just bitter. Last summer, he'd tried opening a Sub Shack in the minimall, and no one had come.

Maybe the patrons of Wenzel's were a little quiet when you saw them around town, the pockmarked men smelling of pipe tobacco, the women with their high, hollow voices and their long hair worn down over their shoulders. But here they were at their ease, grinning at each other across the room from under Tyrolean hats, drinking cheap Milwaukee beer, getting up to stomp and clap their way through the polka. Buck would kick off the set — "And a one and a two and a you know what to do!" — and the Thirty-Pointers stumbled into "Who Stole the Keeshka?" or "That Silver-Haired Daddy of Mine." It was a classic lineup: accordion, clarinet, tuba (of course), two trumpets, snare drum, and acoustic guitar (when the guy showed up). They didn't know what to do, actually, not all of them. Buck and the clarinetist might reasonably be called musicians and could be counted on for a solo each in most tunes, and, as the night went on, sometimes two or three solos. But the rest of the band, who read off huge stacks of sheet music that kept fluttering to the floor like downed geese, were amateur at best.

It didn't matter. People loved them. They were fathoms below even the cover bands I'd seen at the county fair, and people still loved them. Dad and I sat eating brats, me with my kiddie cocktail, Dad with a bottle of Old Style, watching middle-aged women in lederhosen laughing, shouting, practically kicking their legs over their heads.

It took nearly a month of showing up at Wenzel's before Buck called me up to sit in. I was annoyed by his tardiness—Buck *knew* that I played—not least because the tubist in his band was so god-awful. Ertold. Ertold Brauswitter. A little, sparse-haired man somewhere in his late forties, he seemed overwhelmed by his horn. No matter how he positioned the mouthpiece crook, it was either too high or too low. He scooted around on his chair, trying to get comfortable, his arms wrapped around the tuba like someone trying to slow-dance a water heater. He clammed on every tune, his time was despicable, and he didn't have the breath control to get more than a wobbling, anemic tone out of the horn. In a roomful of immigrants and immigrants' children, he seemed somehow more foreign than the rest, with his frazzled, overgrown sideburns the color of used steel wool, his polyester slacks, and his pumpernickel dark eyes.

Outside Wenzel's, in real life, he pumped gas and worked the register at the Union 76 on Kenosha Road. The kids in town tortured him for sport, paying for Pop Rocks and Big League Chew with pocketfuls of dimes and pennies, then swiping Slim Jims from the big jar as he carefully counted out the coins. He always insisted on counting—it never failed. And if he looked up from making those teetering stacks of coins and caught the kids in the act, he'd erupt into some phlegm-rattling language, the words of his native land bursting from him like soda from a shook-up can.

Ertold didn't get it. There were parts to be played in a small town: slick, wealthy mayor; drunken police chief. Overeducated, sentimental, pushover school principal; hyperathletic, closeted homosexual gym teacher. Wild but good-hearted kids; forbearing gas station attendant who only *pretended* to card when the teenagers who hung around the parking lot, swiping steelies or putting crushed-up glass under car wheels, came crowding inside, hauled a twelve-pack to the register and casually, even suavely, asked for Camel Lights and a Bic. But Ertold would shake his head solemnly, put out a withholding hand. "No. Law is law." That's what he said: "Law is law."

Once a kid drew a swastika and the number 666 on the frosted door of the beer cooler, and Brauswitter went nuts. The older kids all said he was a Nazi, and this confirmed it. Though, thinking back on it, he couldn't have been more than ten during the war. And he wasn't German. Getting into the spirit of polka night, he wore green suspenders to Wenzel's but on those suspenders proudly displayed a little orange, blue, and red pin. Rumania? East Prussia? Slovakia? I associate him now with one of those jumbled ancient lands that faded from American memory after 1945. What brought him to our town? Maybe he'd been sent to an aunt or distant cousin, long dead now, who'd settled here in this European enclave of mid-America. Possibly he was a Jew, exiled by the Holocaust. No one knew. In our town—that wide-open, claustrophobic place where the public faith, Lutheranism, was mild as milk—you buried your true beliefs and history deep under your heavy garments.

Finally, on a Sunday late in September, toward the end of the third set, Buck looked down from the bandstand and beckoned around his red accordion. *Come on up, kid. Play a little.* My nervous fingers had been running scales on my kiddie cocktail glass all night. Now I leapt up, climbed onstage, and wormed to the back through the chairs and music stands. Ertold, still clutching his horn, smiled at me, a thin smile, not friendly, then passed it over—a dinged-up three-valve Selmer with an out-turned bell, not even as good as the horn I rented at school. The valve keys and casings were warm and slippery from his sweaty palms and fingers, and the mouthpiece, even after I wiped it off, tasted of mustard pretzels and cheap cologne.

That first night, looking down at me buzzing my lips and working the valves, Ertold couldn't help himself. He softened for a moment, and in a pantomime of familiarity, laughed and clapped me on the shoulder. I was no threat to him; I was just a kid. "Do not forget," he said deliberately. "*Oom-pah, oom-pah.*" Then he put his fist to his mouth and burped softly into it.

Christ, I said to myself, as if I didn't know how to play a polka.

Soon it became routine: In the third set (then, more and more, as early as the second), Buck would summon me up onstage. He'd call a tune, and I'd race to find it in the mess of sheet music Ertold kept on his stand. Very quickly, after only a month or so, I started to hear the progressions—they were simple enough—and I didn't need the music. I'd take a huge breath and lock time with the snare drum. *Fifth, root. Fifth, root.* To my ears, the band sounded better when I got up to play, or maybe it was just that by that point in the night, their fingers and lips were well lubricated by beer. *Fifth, root. Fifth, root.* To sit alongside these men, so close I could feel the bovine warmth of their wide bodies, could feel the way they strained and labored and lost themselves in their rollicking, flatulent music, could feel almost an equal to them—it gave me some confidence and made it a little easier to get through another lonely week at school: I didn't need to be friends with the trombonists in the wind ensemble, who thought it was so funny and so cool to lob balled-up socks and retainer cases and bologna sandwiches into the bell of my tuba—no, I didn't need them, and they could go straight to hell for all I cared and have a cool little club where they burned and blistered forever like four cool, stupid, acned pigs on a spit. After a bar or two of the polka, I didn't care how sour Ertold's mouthpiece tasted. *Fifth, root. Fifth, root. And then, showing off, a run up the scale.* After the last note, my head swam, my cheeks were flushed with puffing. Then Buck called the next tune—"My Little Sweetheart" or "In Heaven There Is No Beer"—and, miracle, I was allowed to stay up on the bandstand. People were clapping, dancing, calling out prost! They loved me.

"How about this kid?" Buck said that first night, and I knew it was my cue to relinquish the horn to Ertold. "The little fella is something, ain't he?" It was a good time in the night for theatrics. Everyone was whistling and stomping their feet and calling for "Roll Out the Barrel."

Back at the table, Dad put a hand on my knee. "Good job, guy. You're improving, I can tell." I wanted to hear those words from him; still, I was bereft at having to come down from the stage. Dad ordered another kiddie cocktail, another Old Style. He was having a good time. The sight of all those Krauts and Polacks, as he called them, shouting and dancing amused him no end. He let me try a sip of his beer and grinned when I stuck out my tongue—*bleh*. Sometimes I think he and I never got any closer than we did going to see that band.

Ertold came past our table at the end of the set. "Nice work, kid," he said, not to me, but to Dad. "He gives it his all, no doubting about it."

"I think he's getting better," Dad said. I was embarrassed to be seen talking with Ertold, but Dad acted deferential, as if he respected the guy. "Got a few tips for the boy?" And why was he asking for advice? What did Ertold know? I was better than him already.

"Oh, a natural. The kid, he is a natural. If only he practice," Ertold warned. "Make sure he practice all of the time. Every day! The tuba," he said gravely, "it is the anchor. Understand. Solid, must be solid all of the time. Like an anchor."

I nodded to myself. This was true. This was supremely true.

Ertold looked down at me now, and for a moment he couldn't conceal his irritation. I don't expect he much enjoyed being shown up by a twelve-year-old. "And no puffing out your cheeks. You lose power that way. You lose breath!" He sucked his cheeks. "Keep them good, tight."

He was right, but I hated him for it. Obviously, I puffed out my cheeks for effect.

Just then, someone at the bar called Ertold's name and waved him over. Ertold leaned back and twanged his suspenders. His pin trembled like a leaf. (Hungarian? A Magyar? A Gypsy?) He bade us good night, hoped we'd had good fun, and then went off to make his rounds. "I come," he called over to the bar, "I come, I come!"

To my surprise, here at Wenzel's, Ertold was a popular figure. He visited each table in turn, talking with the elderly men in their green huntsman's caps, joshing the little kids who tore around and played hide-and-seek under the tables, even flirting with the mothers. The torment he endured at the Union 76 fell away from him. He didn't stoop or sigh or look at the floor, shaking his head in bewilderment and vexation at the behavior of American teens.

After a few weeks, I noticed that he didn't have one native language, but several. At one table, he spoke German. At another, Polish, Czech . . . Slovak? His English was broken and bizarre, but over those craggy, alien languages, he mounted like an alpinist.

Still, he was too eager. I saw how quickly the smile came to Ertold's face at Wenzel's—too quickly. I saw the way his eyes shone when he clowned with the children, the way he sat with his tuba across his lap during breaks, oiling its valves, greasing its slides, doting on his battered, beloved horn. When he stood jawing away with his bandmates at the bar, little showers of spit came popping out of his mouth. Onstage and off, he rushed. Discipline, detachment, calm—these are the things a true musician requires. When the band started up, Ertold launched himself into the performance, then got tangled in the lines of the song as they marched steadily forward. It made it worse that he kept looking out at the crowd, following the dancers, not the music. And yet, for all his bum notes, no one ever seemed to mind him. Once, I even caught Dad giving Ertold a nod and an encouraging smile as he passed our table on his way back up to the bandstand.

Maybe he thought I should've gotten my fill already. He didn't seem to understand why I kept coming back, why every week I was sitting up front, staring at him. When Dad and I walked through the door, it was always Ertold's eyes I met first—he'd started watching for me, as well—and the look in them was not welcoming.

But more people were showing up on Sunday nights—or maybe it was just getting colder, and you wanted to be snug inside a dark, wood-paneled place like Wenzel's—and I figured word had gotten around: I was a hit. By this point, I was playing half of the second set and nearly all of the third. One night, an old guy gave me a ten-dollar bill, "For music lessons," which I took as a compliment. When I looked out from the bandstand at the crowd, I saw Ertold sitting by himself off to the side, not dancing or clapping along, only running his hands through his thin hair, then carefully rearranging those few strands as if he were about to go up and receive an award.

I improvised on the standard parts, played up an octave, then down in the rumbly depths of the tuba's range. I worked on my flutter tongue, my circular breathing. One night, I made a show of straightening the stack of music on Ertold's stand, then turning it blank-side up, to demonstrate to the competent musicians how I could play by ear.

When I wasn't playing, I sat beside my dad in a posture of constant readiness, staring at Ertold. He couldn't concentrate. He clammed all over the place. Buck always saved "Roll Out the Barrel" for him, even gave him a short solo, which he managed by playing the same jaunty little lick over and over. But now Ertold was messing that up as well. He seemed to shrink into himself. He kept scooting around on his chair, more nervous than when he had to count coins at the gas station. I started bringing the school's horn, arriving with it early in the first set. It sat next to me in its case, a bulky black signal of my intent.

Finally, I stood my ground. Buck called "Roll Out the Barrel," and I stayed put. I hoped Ertold would get the picture — it would make things easier on him if he just gave up — but he was already onstage and hefting up his battered Selmer, which had been lying on the floor next to me like scrap. For a second, I thought we were both going to play the song, an uneasy compromise.

Ertold looked down at me and said wearily, "Okay now, kid. Give yourself a rest now."

One of the trumpet players came to my defense. "Ah, let the squirt play one more." I expected the rest of the band — the clarinetist, at least — to second him, but they were busy tuning their instruments and signaling for more beer. I sat there, unwilling to let go my rightful place. Then I looked out into the crowd and caught Dad's eye. He shook his head, mouthed, "Come on, let's go." Slowly, as if weights were lashed around me, I twisted the mouthpiece out of its crook and slipped it into its soft pouch, then upended my tuba and carried it offstage. Ertold took my chair. He knew to check his tongue, but I could almost hear the words: Law is law, kid.

"Just lay off for a while," Dad said. "You've had plenty of chances to play."

"But I'm *better* than him."

He just shook his head again like somehow that wasn't the point.

"But I am, Dad. *Come on.*"

I couldn't believe he wasn't standing up for me. That's what he was supposed to do. We watched the band play "Roll Out the Barrel," and then I got up in a huff, manhandled my horn out the door, across the road, and into the back of our Buick Century.

Dad decided we should take a break from Wenzel's. He'd just gotten a new job at a fancy hotel on the lake and said he couldn't keep staying up till one in the morning when he had to be at work first thing to put out the complimentary English muffins and the ruby red grapefruit juice. After school, I tried to practice, but the études now seemed boring and pointless. I rode my bike around town or threaded my way through the trails in the back forty, calling out my name—"Tiiiimmmmmmmm!!!"—to whoever was out there to hear it. In the evenings, Dad tried hipping me to the music of his youth, hauling his old LPs out of the attic, drawing the black discs out with reverence, playing me Van Morrison, Harry Chapin, Jefferson Airplane, Cat Stevens. But if it didn't have tuba, I wasn't interested. Over those long, endless, cold, and wet weeks, I didn't relent. I drove him crazy blasting John Philip Sousa on the stereo or conducting along with my favorite tape, *Classical Thunder.* When he got up in the morning, I'd already be standing on the ottoman solemnly leading the orchestra as they lumbered through "Mars, the Bringer of War." God, I wore that tape to warbling. Sometimes I heard Dad wandering the house humming Holst's melody, then cursing to himself when he realized what he was doing.

We ran errands on Saturday. Dad had bribed me with the promise of burgers and milk shakes, but his list kept multiplying. He remembered that he needed a couple screws from Heyer's Hardware to keep the screen door from falling off its hinges again, and then at the bank, where he often had to speak with Joan, the loan officer who'd floated him the cash for his failed restaurant, he got some news he hadn't wanted to hear. (I think they were repossessing the riding lawn mower he loved so much, because three weeks later, it disappeared. Stolen, he said, but nothing ever got stolen in our town. Everyone knew each other too well.) We finally got to the Dairy Ripple, but in his distraction he ordered my burger with mayo, and I refused to eat it. We went to the SuperSaver to buy groceries and flowers to put on Mom's grave. They were already playing Christmas music over the PA. "God Rest Ye Merry, Gentlemen"—good tuba part. I fingered the notes on a tin of Dinty Moore.

"Jesus Christ," Dad muttered to himself, "will it ever stop?" Then he picked a scab on his face, and it started bleeding. That morning, he'd tried teaching me to shave—"Any day now you'll see a little peach fuzz"—and had cut himself badly.

He tore off the bottom half of his shopping list and put it in my hand.

"Here, help me out."

He'd never given me this responsibility before, and I felt the proud duty settle on my shoulders like a heavy robe. I left his side, making my way aisle-to-aisle, feeling little coins of satisfaction drop inside me as I found the Bisquick, the Merkts cheese spread, the Kool-Aid, the cocktail onions. I knew these shelves better than Dad thought I did.

I found him again in the cereal. From the end of the aisle, I saw him with the basket in the crook of his arm, holding something—a box of Pop-Tarts—frowning at it like a parking ticket. I stood there for a minute, two, three minutes, not moving. He just kept staring at that box of Pop-Tarts as the other customers maneuvered around him. I went up to him. "Dad?" He startled, looked down at me with wildness in his eyes, then recovered and with a trembling hand put the Pop-Tarts back on the shelf. My first feeling was disappointment—he never bought me sweet things for breakfast—but then as we were checking out, I realized what I had seen. I had seen him crying. My father, crying. Grief goes so deep you can get lost down there and take forever to find your way back.

Outside, a light rain had started. By the time we got to the cemetery, it was pouring. We sat in the car, watching it curtain down the windshield. "They'll just be ruined," Dad said, holding the flowers upright in his hand like someone arriving for a date. "We should just take them home and put them in a vase. She'd like that, right?" He smiled at me.

"Yeah, I guess she would," I said in my most adult voice. "I *know* she would."

But he was unconvinced, and a moment later ducked out into the rain, knelt before the grave, kissed the wet stone, and ran back. As he started the car and put the heater on blasting, I swore I could see a mist coming off his body.

"All right, guy," he said heartily. "All we need to do now is stop and get some gas."

As we pulled into the Union 76, our headlights swept over the little glassed-in shop, and I saw Ertold at the register, ringing up a farmer in a seed jacket and John Deere cap. Dad pulled into the full-service bay. The farmer came out, held the door for another guy going in. We waited. Ertold looked out at our Buick. He recognized it. After all, it had been parked across from Wenzel's every Sunday for nearly two months running. Inside, the customer was taking his sweet time. Ertold could've run out and started pumping for us, but he waited for the guy.

"Son of a bitch," Dad finally said and pushed himself out of the car. He crabbed around between the car and the pump, jammed the nozzle in with a loud rattle, then got back in, even wetter than before. Behind the glass, Ertold looked out at him and shrugged, as if to say, It's either you or me. The pump clicked off. Dad got out to replace the nozzle, and just then Ertold came running out with his monogrammed shirt tented over his head to take the cash. Dad rolled down the window no more than a crack. Ertold hunched down to look in.

"A real wet one," he said, amiable and apologetic now he saw just how soaked Dad was. He glanced at me. His dark eyes, reflecting light off the wet asphalt, shone like two chestnuts. "It rains like a river, yes?"

Dad drummed his fingers on the steering wheel. "Cats and dogs," he said.

Ertold smiled at this, as if it were some joke he didn't understand. There was a yellow daisy petal stuck to the wet front of Dad's coat. Ertold pointed it out. "A bad day for gardening, yes? Very late for gardening."

Dad didn't answer, just pushed a twenty through the window. Ertold started digging through the money pouch he wore around his waist for change, but Dad waved him off. "Christ, just keep it."

That's when I knew that if I bugged him enough he'd take me back to Wenzel's.

It was a quiet night, but still early. The waitress who worked Sundays was lounging at one of the tables, smoking a cigarette, dropping the ashes into a wax-lined plastic basket that held the remains of a half-eaten Jagerschnitzel. She tied her green apron on and came over to our table.

"A few weeks since we've been seeing you boys."

"I just can't keep him away from here," Dad said, flicking his finger at the school tuba sitting next to us in its case. I was almost exploding with excitement, but Dad was out of sorts. He ordered a beer, and a few minutes later he ordered another.

The band trickled in. I watched the clarinetist warming up, admiring the way his hairy, nimble fingers flitted over the keys. Buck came in carrying his accordion in its massive case. He came over and shook hands with my dad, reached down, and tousled my hair, the fat signet ring he wore catching and tugging for a second.

"We'll see if we can't get him up for a number, okay?" he said. "Maybe in the fourth set, if there's time."

I looked at him skeptically, insulted. *The fourth set?* Dad nudged me under the table.

"Thank you, Mr. Schlachtenhaufen," I said.

The rest of the band arrived. A couple of them looked our way, gave us a wave of recognition. Ertold was last; he came bustling in from the cold, his tuba case held out in front of him so he could fit through the door. He shook hands with his band mates, clapped them on the shoulders, told a joke that I couldn't make out but made the guitarist cover his bad teeth to laugh. Then Ertold saw us. His face dropped. For the sole purpose of not having to look at me, it seemed, he got his Selmer out and started oiling the valves.

The Thirty-Pointers warmed up on "Too Fat Polka," and then, once the patrons started arriving, ramped things up with one they didn't play too often, "Grab Your Balls We're Going Bowling." Buck was in good voice that night, and the Thirty-Pointers were keeping up with him. Even Ertold seemed to have got some of his confidence back, though toward the end of the second set he started to falter. I kept my eyes locked on him the whole hour.

Just as the last song of the set ended, Dad got up. "Guy, I need a smoke." He almost never smoked, only when he'd eaten too much or was going over the bankruptcy forms from his Sub Shack. "Stay here." He crossed the room and disappeared into the haze hanging over the smoking section. I sat looking at the furzed carpet, waiting, waiting for him to come back. Someone sat down heavily beside me.

"It is Timothy," Ertold said. "Hello. You are back again. The curious boy."

He seemed drunk, but at Wenzel's the adults were usually drunk.

"Your father," Ertold began. He cleared his throat. "Your father, I see that he is a kind man. He know how much you like to play. To play the polka. You like to be the anchor, yes?"

I nodded my head yes.

"When I was a boy. Your age. No, a little older." He waved the question away, to say that this was of little importance. "When I was a boy, we did not have songs like these, with such—" he labored over the word—"*ridiculous* names. 'Grabbing your balls.' Of course everyone, they like it. Find it funny, and why not? But when I was a boy, we played . . ." He reeled off a list of song titles in German and Polish, closing his eyes and nodding along as if he still heard distant melodies. He shifted his weight on the chair, adjusted his suspenders. A button on his shirt came undone, and I saw a little eye of pale flesh appear. "You see, it is the music of my people. But no one remember these songs. They just want 'Roll Out the Barrel.' Every night, 'Roll Out the Barrel.'"

"It's a good song," I said. "It has a good tuba part."

Ertold sighed, seeming not to hear me. "Perhaps I practice more. Always practice, that's what I say. But there is no time. Never any time. You will be good, I know. You will be very good tuba." His eyes took me in now, really looked at me. "But for now, the polka for adults. For the older people."

He waited for me to answer him.

"My sister," Ertold went on, "to see my sister dance the polka. Oh, such a dancer! My sister, my mother, my father, my brother. They could dance, yes, but none of them could play!" He shook his head, smiled sadly. "I was the only musical one in the family." He laughed at something, himself or the memory of his family, I couldn't say. "So, for adults only, understand?"

It would've taken something I didn't possess at that age to see how much all this meant to sad old Ertold, how badly he needed to be up there playing. Anyway, I didn't have it. I couldn't see: When his gaze wandered out across the crowd, distracted, forgetting the music, it wasn't my eyes he was seeking.

Buck loomed over our table. "I see you two trading notes over here." He rested a hand on Ertold's shoulder. "Come on, time to finish out the night." He looked at me. "Maybe we can get the little guy up for a couple numbers, all right? Just a couple."

Ertold sat there, stiff under Buck's restraining hand. "A couple of songs," he muttered. "Of course. It is your group." He rose from the chair — Buck's hand still on his shoulder, then releasing him — and went to the bar for another beer.

I looked up at Buck. "I'm ready to play whenever."

"Well, he sure don't lack enthusiasm," Buck said about me, but not to me.

Ertold stood at the bar, watching us sullenly. Buck turned his back on me for a moment. Just then, staring right at Ertold, I took a big breath and puffed out my cheeks.

Ertold's mouth came open. The color drained from his face. He seemed about to speak but instead put the bottle of Old Style to his lips, sucked a drink, then hurriedly crossed the room and disappeared down the back corridor leading to the bathrooms and the kitchen.

The band reconvened onstage for their last set, but Ertold wasn't there. Buck said his name on the microphone, made a joke about nature's call. Ertold didn't show. Buck looked around the bar once more, puzzled, then halfheartedly sang out, "And a one and a two and a you know what to do," and the Thirty-Pointers started playing without Ertold, the music sounding hollow and inert without a low part to fill things out.

Dad came back. He had cigarettes he'd bummed from someone, one behind each ear. He sat drumming his fingers on the table, out of time with the rhythm, not even watching the band. He stood up again.

"Come on, we have to go."

"We're leaving?" This was finally my chance to take over for good. "There's no one to play tuba."

"They'll survive. Come on. Let's get out of here. Time to go."

The band was starting up "In Heaven There Is No Beer" as we walked out. A few people were clapping and singing along, even though the music was so empty sounding.

Outside, the temperature had dropped, and the cold air stung my lips. Dad crossed the road. I lagged behind, held back by the weight of my horn, but I saw it first. Near the rear wheel of our Buick Century, a dark figure crouched. When he heard us coming, he jumped up.

"What the fuck?" Dad said, startled. Then his voice got cautious. "Okay, take it easy, take it easy. We're going. We're out of here, okay?"

In his left hand Ertold held the end of a broken bottle. For a moment, I believed he was going to kill my father. Then I saw what he'd been doing: putting crushed-up glass under our tire. "You fucking Nazi!" I shouted, cursing because Dad had, and I thought it was allowed.

The commotion had brought some of the patrons of Wenzel's outside, and now more joined them. Ertold stood there holding the jagged bottle by its neck as everyone looked on. "This little boy!" he said, gesturing at me. "Can't you see? He . . . He . . ." In his broken English, it came out sounding so childish. "He make fun of me!"

No one answered him. They were appalled. This kind of behavior was foreign to them. It was the way Americans acted. Someone had summoned the band members outside. Ertold stood there, dark eyes imploring them, asking for justice, the wisps of his hair rising up, drifting in the cold wind. A long time seemed to pass before the clarinetist came carefully over, almost on tiptoe, and quietly said something to Ertold in German. He eased the bottle from Ertold's hand, and then Buck came over as well, and he and the clarinetist took Ertold inside. After a few confused moments, the crowd followed, closing ranks behind the three men. Buck came out to speak to us. He fumbled out an apology on Ertold's behalf, but I could tell all he wanted was to get us out of there. Dad and I got in the Buick and drove home in silence. *Classical Thunder* was sitting on the seat next to me, but I knew not to put it in.

That little town seems so distant to me now—flat, featureless, and as distant as a dreamland where everyone sleeps and never wakes. But back then it was filled with charm, strange tradition, local marvels. You only had to look hard enough.

The Thirty-Pointers played a few more times, without Ertold. But the mood was ruined, and the Sunday-night crowd silted away. I hoped Buck might call one day and ask me to join, but I guess he couldn't keep a twelve-year-old out all night in a bar, even if he wanted me. The band broke up. At the restaurant, Buck played the same, familiar tunes solo, but the sight of a large man playing a red leather accordion suddenly seemed comical rather than festive.

For weeks, the kids in town were full of rumors about Ertold— he heard voices, he tortured animals, somewhere back there in the old country he had fifteen bodies buried—but eventually the talk died down and people forgot exactly what had happened. That fall, having skipped a grade, I went up to the high school, a school of a thousand that bussed kids in from all over. I auditioned for Honors Orchestra, but I'd stopped practicing and wasn't even good enough to make third chair.

Two months later, there was an accident. Three senior boys were driving to a rock concert, drunk out of their skulls. At a lonely intersection way out in the country, the driver blew a stop sign and plowed straight into the broadside of a semi. There were big grainy photos of the two boys who died printed in the local paper, a huge memorial service at the Lutheran church, counselors and psychologists crawling all over the school. It was the kind of accident that, briefly, brings a community together.

Some of the mothers from the booster club, after a little detective work, traced the beer back to the Union 76. The boy who survived the accident said Ertold had sold it to them. They had fake IDs — terrible, homemade fake IDs — but he hadn't even bothered to check.

A petition was drawn up, but Ertold quit before he could be fired. He moved away, God knows where. Around town, Ertold's name didn't come up often (Why would it? Only the Krauts and the Polacks really knew him), but whenever anyone talked about him, it was always said that he'd finally gone back home.

When I turned fourteen, I started working at the SuperSaver bagging groceries, saving my paychecks for my first drum set. From the day I brought it home, I spent every minute I had down in the basement with headphones on, playing along to jazz records. Dad couldn't understand this cerebral, uncompromising music I now preferred — nor, I suppose, did I want him to. He saw me losing myself in my new obsession but didn't dare intrude. In this way, another long Wisconsin winter went by, and he and I learned to be strangers.

Power
Ballads

It's worse than dating, I told Kate. Every band you join, every job you take, it's always the same: That first awkward jam, feeling each other out, trying to play it cool — and then at the end of the night, *Hey, great to meet you, man. Sounded rockin'.* The deadly pause. *So, want to try this again?* Both sides wondering, Am I better than this? Can I even stand to be around these bozos? And if you do it a second time, a third, the expectations, the planning. Everyone wants to know if your dreams are their dreams. *Yeah, we'll start off playing the smaller clubs, lay down a demo, work some industry contacts, do the festival circuit, maybe go over to Europe . . .* You just nod your head, tell them you're committed, 100 percent, you want to make this thing happen. But the whole time you're calculating when to bail. A loser will drag you down quick. You've got to keep your options open or—

"So, that's you idea of dating?" Kate and I had been going about six months at that point, and we were still bright and reckless with one another, still taunting, still teasing. "Were you thinking all that when you met me?"

"Well, don't take it literally. Bands and girls aren't *exactly* the same thing."

"Oh, fantastic. You always know the right thing to tell me, Timmy boy."

I told her I loved her, that the moment we met eyes in that dive bar in Rogers Park, all my petty hang-ups fluttered away.

"So we're just talking every other girl you've dated, then?"

"Jesus, no . . . that's not what I'm saying." And then to explain—to *try* to explain—I told her about Billy Sakura and his band Soldier.

When I first came to the city I was a whore. I'd take any gig I could get. I'd just finished at North Texas—four years practicing my ass off to hold down the drum chair in the One O'clock Band—and I was ready to prove I was a pro, that there wasn't a job out there I couldn't nail. In truth, I was living for those fire-breathing sessions on the north side—all the cats packed into the Bottle, Hungry Brain, the Velvet, just tripping out all night, orbiting in atmospheres too rarified for common consumption—but good luck trying to make that music pay. "Must be a reason they call it 'free' jazz," my dad said every time I tried to hip him to my music. So, I took the singer-songwriter gigs, the cover-band gigs, the weddings, the cocktail jobs. I was paying my dues. Sleeping in my practice space when I couldn't make rent, living off Easy Mac and Korean hot noodles—oh, yes, I believed I was doing it the authentic way, that I wasn't just another white kid from the sticks trying to hang. I believed I was earning my soul, my right to play.

The flyer had been up at Azarello's, where I went for my equipment, for months:

The Return: SOLDIER. Hard-hitting, shred-head rock-N-roll.
Need INSANE drummer. Sticksmen! are you ready to roll out
the big guns??? We've got songs. We've got gigs. All we need is
you. Must be 1000% committed. No bullshit, no egos, no pos-
ers, no jobbers.

I remembered them, barely—a last-gasp eighties band that had lingered into the nineties like a stubborn stain before being erased by grunge and "alternative." Soldier—the kind of stuff that mechanics and construction workers cranked before Bears games, that ruled the day back when quarterbacks wore their hair long. They'd had a minor hit somewhere toward the end, one of those lumbering, heart-on-sleeve ballad turns that traded on working-class pride and memories of a girl lost to the ravages of war. "DMZ of Love." My dad was a child of the seventies, but that song always got him. He used to turn it up whenever it came on WKIS.

Only one tab on the flyer was torn off (the tab the poster had torn off, of course). No one in the city was clamoring for the Return. The city had gone post/avant everything. No one even wanted to think about bands like Soldier. It was just too embarrassing. Maybe I called the number out of some perverse curiosity. Maybe it was because I remembered my dad humming tunelessly along to the guitar solo in "DMZ." Maybe it was those two beautiful words: "Got gigs."

We jammed for the first time in Billy's garage down in Blue Island. I felt good, calm, collected, in control. "You've done your homework, kid," Billy said after the first couple songs. "Not bad." I'd found three of their albums in the used bin of a record shop. Hard-driving, heavy blues-rock with the shuffles straightened out, lots of sixteenth-note fills, an odd bar thrown in here and there, some tricky right-hand right-foot ostinato—grist for the practice-room mill. Otherwise: plenty of lead guitar, lots of shrieking and double entendres, Catholic guilt and terror, and pre-adolescent lizard-brain boner jokes. This music had pogoed back and forth between the American suburbs and the steel towns of northern England so much it had become almost a continent of its own, its citizens loyal, unbathed, and still not convinced the singer from Judas Priest was actually gay.

We played a few more rockers, then Billy ended the audition.

"Hang out awhile, kid. Drink a few brews." He popped me a can of Bud Light Ice. It was all they drank. Billy, Carlos, and Arne—they'd formed Soldier back in high school—thirty years and three beer-guts later they'd decided to mount a counterattack against aging gracefully. "The three of us are gonna step out for a minute and confer."

When they came back in, I could tell they were excited. They were playing it cool, but I could tell. They'd tried out a handful of drummers over the last six months, but I was the first one, Billy said, who'd brought "some respect" to their music. He popped another round of Buds. I couldn't help myself. I stayed and got drunk. We jammed till the neighbors called the cops. Those old dudes could wail. They were exact, reverent; they were like their own tribute band. Loading up my drums at the end of the night, I couldn't remember when I'd had this kind of dumb fun. "Tim," Billy said, pushing a bag of clothes into my arms, "here you go." Inside was a set of olive green fatigues.

"What's this?"

"You're infantry, kid. A grunt. Welcome to the band."

"You had a *costume*?"

"Well, that's why they were Soldier." Carlos had an air force flight suit and mirrored shades. Arne wore navy dress whites and a doughboy cap. Billy was the samurai. He had a belted robe, rope sandals, his hair back in a ponytail. He played a Flying V he'd had customized back in '85 to look like a katana sword. "He was Japanese American," I explained. "Onstage he went by his mother's maiden name."

"Jesus Christ, you're describing the Village People."

"Well, no, I mean, this was serious. Soldier was mostly serious. That's what made them great. A straight face was the only way they could pull it off."

Kate laughed, though not cruelly. It was getting late, and we'd taken our drinks into the bedroom. She was waiting to see where

I was going with all of this. We tumbled down on the bed. "This was important to you, wasn't it?" She reached over and started playing with my hair, the way she always did when she couldn't tell what I was thinking.

Before our first gig: a few full-band rehearsals and a lot of time shedding the songs by myself. Billy had some old contacts among the local promoters. We were booked at Champs, in the far suburbs, down where Chicagoland begins to exasperate with its concrete ceaselessness. The place was a cavern, eclipsed only by the Six-Flags-Over-Jesus megachurch down the strip and the old packing plant that squatted in abandonment across the tracks. I was used to dim little coffee shops where skinny dudes sat stroking goatees and uttering the occasional soft *unh* of approval at the end of solos, a sound that always made me think of them tangled up, sweating in bed with their stick-legged, asthmatic girlfriends.

The crowd at Champs—and, Jesus, was there a crowd—were south-siders, that particular strain of midwesterner whose Polish or Irish blood has thinned to an obscure murmur in the veins that requires them to eat pierogi or corned beef and cabbage once a year and to migrate in droves. But as I looked around, it wasn't just white dudes: some pudgy Mexican guys, a cluster of Asian cats—friends of Carlos and Billy, I guessed, or maybe butt rock is simply the great blue-collar leveler. Hell, there were even some *women* in the audience. At the bar, they stood toying with their hoop earrings and spritzed curls, smoking slims. The smell of menthol filled the room. Twenty years melted away. On a dim big-screen TV, Jim McMahon floated a winning pass to Willie Gault and the world-champion Bears did the Super Bowl shuffle.

The lights went down. A spot swept across the stage and came to rest where the four of us stood in staggered silhouette, me struggling to keep from falling to one knee. In place of the flag we raised Billy's katana/guitar.

"Oh God," Kate said, "like the Iwo Jima memorial?"

"Well, that was the idea anyway."

The crowd thundered. Hoots, hollers, and plenty of catcalls. We broke formation, and Billy dived into the riff to "Iron Curtain."

I beat hell out of my drums, four long years of studied restraint erased in the rush of vicarious nostalgia. Billy had made me get a buzz cut, and sweat poured down my face. My helmet kept slipping down over my eyes, and my fatigues, which were a size too small, cut me under the pits. But I was delirious, grinning stupidly, ready to bust out laughing the whole hour and a half. At the end of the night, Billy put five hundred bucks in my hand.

"Comeback city," he drawled in his thick south-side accent. He knocked a Kool out of a softpack, dangled it under his upper lip. The night had gone as well as anyone could've hoped, though I'd seen him pacing in the alley before the crowd started arriving. "That's some good playing tonight, kid. You're a real quick learner." He reached back and let down his ponytail. His thick, dark hair framed his face and spread over his shoulders. He suddenly resembled the guy on the covers of those old albums—fleshily handsome, dissolute, intimidating. "Now alls we got to work on is 'DMZ.'"

"Why, what's wrong with it? It's the easiest song in the book."

He sucked his Kool down to the filter, looked at me calmly but impatiently. "That's the one they're waiting to hear, ain't it? Couldn't you see it out there, see them waiting?" Someone came up and asked him to sign a copy of *Battle of the Bulge*. He whipped off an autograph, sent the guy away with a silent nod. In front of the fans he never broke character. He was inscrutable, stoic, depthless. He was the samurai. You'd never have known that by day he did tax preparation. "That's the song gotta connect. That's the one gotta *hit*. It's a power ballad. You know what that means, don't you?"

It wasn't exactly on the curriculum in Music History. "Sure, I know what you're talking about." Sensitive acoustic strumming and lardy fat backbeats, falsetto harmonies, a hammer-on drenched solo soaring like Icarus with his wings dripping off—the power ballad was the part of the show when, for some reason, everyone but the drummer sat on high stools. I pictured a darkened arena, fifty thousand lighters held aloft, bobbing up and down on an ocean of schlock. "My dad used to love 'DMZ,'" I said.

"Shit, you write a hundred songs, and that's the one they all remember."

He said it for the sake of appearances. He wasn't bitter about being a one-hit wonder. He played all of his songs with pop-eyed urgency, legs spread wide, lips glued to the mic, but for "DMZ," he bowed his head and submitted, as if the music were coming through him and he was simply the conduit, the sluice, the terrestrial receiver.

"A hundred to one. Those aren't bad odds when you think about it."

"Lot better than some guys do." He inserted another smoke under his lip. "So, how's this going? This a good fit for you—playing with three old guys like us?"

I hesitated. This was the moment to bow out, no hard feelings. I thought of the cash in my pocket. "I'm having a blast."

He clapped me on the shoulder, and I felt his gratitude and his approval shiver up and down my spine. "No point if you ain't having fun!" I was giving him what he wanted, wasn't I? A little taste of former glory—a short, stiff dram of the stuff that tells us we can go on forever. Billy ordered shots. We raised them up. He winced as he took his down.

We sat at the bar while they closed the place up. Billy talked about his father, who'd been stationed at Okinawa after the war and played electric guitar in the base band, covering whatever was on the jukebox back home for the airmen and their wives: Chuck Berry, Carl Perkins, Link Wray—learning from his dad had been a history lesson on all the hottest guitarists from way back.

I shook my head. "My dad cut town just after I got my scholarship to music school. He went out west. Last I heard he was living with some woman and selling those customized mouse pads with your own photo printed on them. About all he and I ever had in common was our eyes, hair, and Fleetwood Mac."

Billy put his arm over my shoulders, pulled me in tight. He smelled of beer and Aqua Velva. "Well, that's a hell of a lot right there." I guess I sounded more torn up about it than I meant to.

"Yeah," I said, "they were a beautiful band."

We played Rascal's, Pine Lodge, Jakers, the casinos over in Hammond. We had a draw. The people remembered Soldier. They brought their wives, their girlfriends, their zitty teenage kids.

Down here in the crotch of Lake Michigan, they were starved for spectacle. I looked out at the entire front row head-banging, pinwheels of greasy hair, guys pumping their fists, coiling into themselves like they were about to break boards. I took some of my gig money and plunked it down on a new kit, a ten-piece monstrosity that, up in the city, I was ashamed to be seen packing into my van. It had two kick drums. Billy got me new skins for them, one emblazoned with "Sold" and the other with "-ier." Arne with his electric bass slung low, laboring with it like he was swabbing deck; Carlos leaning back in his stance, kinky hair down to his ass, staring up at the lights through mirrored Aviators, wailing through solo after solo, standing at attention, saluting—how could I forget that time? When I had the helmet and fatigues on, I was someone else. I wasn't meditating on the difference between postbop and hard bop or the evolution of the sacred *naningo* rhythm of West Africa; I wasn't getting up on a coffeehouse stage just to cut some other cat, make him wish he'd never picked up a pair of sticks. Maybe I'd ruined myself with all that practice, all that high seriousness, trying to be Tony Williams, Elvin Jones, Idris Mohammed. "You can only be one person in this world," my dad always told me. I'd always figured it was just what he said to excuse his fuck-ups.

We were on break one night. I was at the bar with Arne. He was shy, smiled a lot, didn't say much. But he wore that sailor outfit with pride, without self-consciousness. Over the last couple weeks, I'd come to learn that Arne harbored a secret love for pop classical: "Ride of the Valkyries," "In the Hall of the Mountain King," that sort of stuff. We started talking favorite composers. His was Leonard Bernstein. Me, I liked Pierre Boulez.

"Maybe we should record an album with the CSO," Arne said. He only seemed to be half-joking.

"I always thought there should be a death metal band that only played the Austro-German romantics," I told him. "They'd be called Mauler. Get it?"

"Nah," Arne said, shaking his head, "it'd never work."

Billy was out back in the alley readying himself for the next set. Until the end of the night, he was unapproachable. Carlos came over, and I bought him a drink. He and I were getting to be buddies, I thought. We still had to warm up the conversation a little, compliment each other on our playing. He told me that, technically, I was light years beyond their original drummer, Jens. "You remind me of a Mexican Jimi Hendrix," I said. Flattery makes me generous, but he really was a fine guitarist—entirely self-taught, a natural. He had the chops, the ear; he even still had the hair. In his genre, he could've played with pretty near anyone.

"Billy's been riding me," I confided in Carlos. "Says I haven't been playing 'DMZ' right." Fifteen gigs in, and apparently I still wasn't getting it. Professionally, I was irked.

"Don't worry about him. He's a perfectionist. He wants it be like it was, acts like he's happy playing these bars, but, hell, he's having his midlife crisis, like we all are." Carlos waxed philosophical: "I don't know, maybe people are digging this because it's so blatant—three old dudes pretending they're teenagers. It's completely shameless. People respond to that. We played Soldier Field back in the day. We opened up for Ratt. That was, you know, our zenith, our Thermopylae." He killed his beer, tossed his hair off his shoulders with a shake of his head. "They booked us because of the name."

Even with all their hard work and *esprit de corps*, Carlos went on, Soldier was never more than a local favorite. Their renown hadn't taken them farther than Kansas City or Milwaukee, playing daylight slots at Summerfest, pumping up the crowd for the main attraction. At that point, they were all in their thirties. They didn't have to be the guys who hung out with movie stars and dated supermodels. They could be the guys who hung out with the Bears' kicker (and sometimes even the defensive line), who dated the gals who worked the auto show and made appearances for Bud Light Ice, who maybe, after a few years, asked one of those gals to get hitched.

"We were kinda proud of what we'd achieved, you know? Maybe that's why it was so hard for Billy to take."

Just after the big news came, the incredible, pop-the-champagne-and-dance-on-tables-till-the-cops-show-up news—they'd been tapped to go on a nationwide and European tour as part of the lineup that had played Soldier Field—Billy's wife, Denisa, held the little cardboard tube up to the bathroom light and watched it turn blue. It was the inevitable turn of events. To his credit, Billy made the right decision; he was going to be there to see little baby

Shayla come into the world, learn to crawl, learn to speak, play her first power chord. Hell, he wasn't going to be out there committing ritual *seppuku* at the end of every set, night after night, just to please an arena's worth of fans who weren't even there to see them anyway. Soldier canceled the tour, split the band fund four ways. Billy put the cash toward a down payment on the house in Blue Island.

But there were complications. Little baby Shayla never left the hospital; then Denisa got real sick afterward. As Ratt rampaged across the Eastern Seaboard and Europe, Billy was burying his daughter. "I think Billy got caught up in a certain amount of regret," Carlos told me, "maybe a certain amount of resentment too." He should've known better, but it was a tough time. It got pretty bad between him and Denisa, and when the two of them finally made a clean break, Carlos and Arne were already raising their own kids, Jens was back in Stockholm, it was 1990, and Soldier was just a faint, stale odor on the shifting winds of local adulation.

"But then you had 'DMZ.' That was a triumph, right?"

"For us, that was really more a farewell thing. Billy had a few songs lying around. We flew over and hooked up with Jens for a month. *The Sweden Sessions*. We barely broke even on that record. For Billy," Carlos said, "the idea was always we were gonna come back. I never really believed him." He raised a shot, drank it down. "But what else you gonna do when the cars are paid off, the kids are in school, and you've redecorated the house five times already? I mean, why the fuck not, right?"

I took my shot, winced. "Right."

As we stood leaning at the bar, a guy came in. It was that time of the night when the doorman, already drunk, would let anyone in. The guy looked like a Soldier fan. He wore camo pants and a sleeveless undershirt. Over his shoulders, a bright green python was draped like a mink stole. As he came through the crowd, people parted to make way, then gathered in to pet it. "They like a spectacle," I said to Carlos. The python's head bobbed near the guy's mouth as people stroked its shiny scales; the guy leaned over to feel its forked tongue flicking over his stubble. Someone must have said, How long is that thing anyway? because the guy laid it out on the pool table, grandly, to demonstrate its length and girth. Of course the first thing it did was disappear down the corner pocket, and then all the numb-nuts who'd gathered round had a contest of intellects to see who could get the damn thing out. No one wanted to stick their hand in the pockets for fear of getting bitten. Someone suggested slotting some quarters in and racking up a game—that would get the fucker out of there PDQ. The guy looked wounded, truly bereft. He had some snake food out in his truck and tried to coax his baby out with a few pellets smeared on the butt end of a cue. The bartender came over with a flashlight and, holding his head away, tried peering down each of the pockets. It looked like they were going to have to take the whole table apart. But, then, just as we were about to play our second set, the snake's tiny head popped out—from the same pocket it had gone into—looked this way and that like a periscope hunting a convoy. The guy in camo pants leaned over; the snake flicked its tongue out, feeling for his chin; the guy grabbed it behind its head and yanked it out of the pocket.

"Fuck me," I said, shaking my head, "what a fucking hick."

Arne stood there, aloof in his sailor suit. "Ah, that's just my cousin," he said.

The snake coiled around the guy's neck like it would choke the life out of him, but he didn't flinch; that was the trust between them, that was the—

"I think you're getting a little sidetracked with this snake thing."

"No, no, the snake is the entire point. I mean, this guy loved his snake, unreservedly. Pure devotion."

"Well, everyone has to find meaning somewhere."

"He loved the band too. He came to our next five shows."

Kate and I started fooling around. I unknotted the drawstrings of her pajamas. She batted my hand away. "At ease, Private."

"Hey—"

"That's sad, about Billy. Billy Sakura," she said, trying his name out.

"I find it kind of inspiring, actually. He never gave up."

She rolled her eyes. "Oh, give me a break."

We started stripping off our clothes. Kate kissed me roughly, but then she pulled back. "Say we go the distance, you and me. Someday I might ask you to get a steady job. Be a band teacher maybe. What would you say to that?"

I was annoyed. This wasn't right. This was supposed to be the kind of late-night intimacy where you tell your lover a sad story and expect to be either absolved of your minor sins or to be fucked, hopefully both.

"I'd consider reasonable arguments." I thought we might still be joking around, so I threw out an improbable: "I'd move to Nashville, put on a cowboy hat, do studio work."

Kate's mouth turned down. She was upset. "Why do you always think you're missing out on your real life?"

"Because I'm never satisfied. That's why you love me, right?"

She didn't answer. She tucked herself under the covers, away from my searching fingers. "So, what happened?" she said. "Where is this going anyway?"

A few weeks after the snake, I drove down to Blue Island for rehearsal.

"Where's Arne? Where's Carlos?"

"Just you and me today." Billy had his acoustic out. He was sitting on a high-backed barstool strumming lightly, meditating. "Thought we'd work on 'DMZ.'"

He began to play the song, softly, as if to remind himself how it went. I sat behind the kit and played some warm-up exercises on the fleshy part of my thigh, Swiss triplets: LRRLLRRL RLLRRLLR.

Billy began to sing. His voice had gone ragged from all those years screaming over amplifiers. Still, it had a gruff sort of sweetness, a barrelhouse melodrama. Tough and theatrical—that was the power ballad formula.

The first verse was a grab bag of metaphors, with lines from an antacid commercial: "Something is happening / deep down inside." Then the fog of war drifted in—distant rumbling, a flickering blaze on the horizon, a lone cry of anguish (far-off electric howls from Carlos). A girl is running, a beautiful girl with her long, dark hair strewn out behind her. She has been crying, but cries no longer. She stumbles, she stands again. This was the part of the song when my dad always reached over to turn up the volume, when he went flush and seemed a little stricken. (After all, who values defiance more than those who are already beaten?) In a song like this, it was unusual to hold out so long for the chorus. The girl was still running, still striving, survival her only dream; she was there, almost there, safety, warmth, her lover's arms not just a taunt but a promise. And then—*"The sound of drums and guns will shake the earth!"*—my cue, and I came in on the toms with holy thunder, crashed into the downbeat, and started laying it down with the smiling conviction of a Vegas magician, a gentleman bank robber, a serial killer, a lying politician, utterly drunk on my own mastery.

Billy stopped playing. He sat there looking at me. "Maybe we should do a couple beers first." He went to the fridge and brought out two cans. He moved his guitar from the stool to its stand, put the cold can to his forehead, sighed. "How about a tour?"

"I'm open to it, you know, if the money's right." I wasn't sure a tour was the best thing for Soldier at this point, or how long these guys would even hold up on the road. It seemed like Billy was being a little wistful, like he was taking this comeback thing a little too seriously. There was no sense in disinterring the past, trying to make it walk again. It was dangerous, foolish. Still, I tried to be equable. "Hell, I'd do it for the professional experience."

"I meant a tour of the house."

"Oh, sure."

I'd never been inside Billy's home, always the garage. "So, this is the downstairs." A lot of time had passed; you could just barely see a woman's touch in the faded curtains, the harvest-themed tablecloth, the fancy stenciling on the baseboards. The living area had long ago lapsed into functionality: multitiered rack of stereo equipment, a bookshelf jammed with old LPs, a weight bench with tax law manuals stacked on it. Billy grabbed another beer. He was like a cracked radiator—just keep adding fluid.

"I don't mind doing taxes," he said. "Keeps me sharp, all that math. Math and music—Siamese twins, right? Anyways, it gives me plenty of time to practice guitar. I'm my own boss."

We padded up the carpeted stairs in our socks. The ceilings were high, the hallway narrow, walls the color of mayonnaise. There was a landing, a Jacuzzi bathtub, a skylight. Faux grand. Twenty years ago, they'd built a zillion of these houses. For a lot of people, this was the exact shape and dimensions of their dreams. If my dad had ever been able to hang on to a job longer than six months, I would've grown up in a house just like this.

In the master bedroom: a huge TV, waterbed, guitars hanging from pegs—prototypes of the katana. There didn't seem to be a single picture in the whole place. Under the guitars, a low shelf with cassette tapes in chronological order—demos—and several larger square boxes of reel-to-reel tape, labeled "Sweden," "Bulge," "The Gods of War," "Cannon Fodder," and "unreleased." There appeared to be a lot of unreleased material.

I had to admire the simplicity of his life, the single-minded-ness. After tax season, he had nothing to do but spend all day with his guitar and his four-track recorder. We went back out into the hallway. There was one last room, the only door that had been closed. Billy led me inside. The shades were drawn, but in the dim light I could see a pile of stuffed animals, a mobile of stars hanging from the ceiling, a high-railed crib still made up neatly. The room smelled not of dust but clean, fresh, like someone had put down carpet stuff. As my eyes adjusted, I saw among the stuffed bears four human dolls, handmade and a little misshapen, but faithful in likeness: a sailor, a fighter ace, a GI, a samurai with long, flowing hair.

"I was always pretty good with needle and thread," Billy said softly. If not for his meat-hook accent, those words might have been beautiful. I picked up the GI, held it up next to me. "Any resemblance?" I said.

"Must have known you'd come along one day."

We went back downstairs and ran through "DMZ" together. In jazz, a ballad is all restraint. You play the melody so it sounds a little shaky, a little battered. You work, you study to be older, wiser, so that you can play it from a distance, thirty years at least. Jazz knows that experience trumps all, that you take the blows as they come. "DMZ of Love" was five and a half minutes of end-less protest, of standing at the crumbling edge of the ocean un-der the bright sobbing moon, howling and tearing your hair. The girl climbs to the top of the cliff, looks across the water, turns to survey the wreckage behind her, the impossibilities she has surmounted. "And though the guns have faded," Billy sang, "still she roams and battles on. / Maybe one day we'll meet her / in the land beyond the sun." We played it again and again, just the two of us. I played with my eyes closed, made it look like I was dredging my soul. One last time—I went for the final chorus, threw everything at it, Billy played the five-note melody, the last note rang out forever in that echoing garage. I opened my eyes. He was looking at me. I nodded my head slowly, meaningfully, and so did he. "Like that," he said softly. "Just like that."

I felt nothing, absolutely nothing. All I was thinking was LRLLRR LRLLRR and RLRLRRRLLL RLRLRRRLLL and RRRLLL RRRLLL and, of course, LLRRLLRR LLRRLLRR. I packed up my equipment. Just as I was leaving, Billy drew something out of his pocket.

"Here."

"What's this?"

"Your stripes." He paused. "Sergeant."

I took the patch from him. It, too, was hand-sewn.

"And then what happened?" Kate said. I'd fallen quiet; I didn't feel like telling the story anymore.

"I had to quit. It was getting too depressing."

"But you got there, right? You finally played the song. You gave him what he wanted."

"Yeah, but I quit."

I couldn't even bring myself to do it in person. I called Billy up, gave him the one excuse I knew he'd go for. "It's my dad. He's sick." I mumbled something about a heart condition. "I'm going out to Oregon to see him."

Billy didn't answer for a moment.

"Family comes first," he finally said.

"I can get you a sub. I know plenty of guys who can nail this job."

"No jobbers," Billy said. "This is a band."

Kate started playing with my hair again. She thought this was the point of the story, the thing that had kept me up nights. "Well, Soldier wasn't you," she said. "You're a jazz musician." When she saw that I wasn't going to accept her assurances so easily, she said,

"So, will you ever be satisfied? That's what we've been talking about, right, you and me?"

"Yeah." I hesitated, fatal hesitation. "You and me." I got up, went over to the stereo, put a record on. Sonny Rollins, *The Bridge*. "I love you," I said. We'd only been saying those words for a week or so. They still seemed foreign to me, and I spoke them uncertainly, as if I might unknowingly be making a fool of myself. We went to bed and lay in each other's arms and listened to Sonny's tenor blowing disconsolately over "Where Are You?" while Jim Hall fretted coolly in the background and Ben Riley caressed his snare and cymbals. I couldn't help humming along.

"Don't go disappearing into this record like you do with your drum exercises. Tell me what you were going to tell me."

I looked her right in the eyes. "I guess it's just like anything. You have to find the right fit." We kissed again. "Just tell me you're not going to hurt me."

"No guarantees." But she saw that I needed more. "If you don't hurt me."

I reached up, turned off the light, and pulled her to me.

I wasn't telling her the out-and-out truth. After that last re-hearsal, I did play a few more gigs with Soldier, still trying to work myself up to having to break Billy's heart.

We were back at Champs. It was just another night. I was feeling loose, going for things I wouldn't normally, shanking a few of them. We played "Cannon Fodder," "Iron Curtain," "Deployment Princess (You're Still Ugly Back Home)." I was riding on muscle memory; I had the entire set under my hands, and my helmet stuffed with newspaper so it wouldn't slip. The lights went down. Billy took up his acoustic. I focused on that one thing, that five-note melody. Carlos's guitar howled in the background, but Billy raised a hand to say, Another time around. We sat there, vamping, letting the atmosphere get heavy. Billy never took his eyes off me. He knew. He knew I was leaving.

We played the verse and the chorus, and then, finally, the solo. Arne closed his eyes, concentrating on the bass line, the fat strings rumbling under his delicate fingers. Carlos leaned back, his hair glistening with sweat, his guitar climbing and climbing, floating up there like a rocket aiming for heaven. Billy came off his stool and crouched low, cradling his acoustic.

In the crowd, a tiny, flickering light bumped my concentration. I faltered for a moment, looked down at the skin of my snare drum and saw wet blotches on it. I met Billy's eyes again, but his told me, No, out there, look out there.

In the darkness, the crowd swayed together, lighters held aloft. Another tiny light sparked, then another. One by one they all came on.

Heart of
Hearts: ★★★½

*Fans of melancholy take note. On her debut ef-
fort, Hol Perry, former native of the gray-belt ghostland surrounding Detroit, turns in a twelve-song set steeped in the grand
tradition of American poverty, heartache, and decay. In part a
chronicle of Perry's flight from the barren womb of industrial-
capitalism to the more robust (and musically vital) Chicago,*
Heart of Hearts *is the sound of one artist struggling in solitude
to cast off a stifling legacy of pain.*

They played Tuesdays, for beer and tips, to a near-empty bar.
There were nights that winter when only Kate, Holly's best friend
and roommate, was out there listening. She didn't make every

Tuesday, but she made most of them, enough so she knew every song Holly and her band covered. Emmylou Harris, Joni Mitchell, the Carter Family—they preferred the classic stuff, though Holly sang newer artists, too: Steve Earle, Gillian Welch, Keaton Wilding.

Holly and her band—Patrick on bass and Billy on banjo, fiddle, and musical saw—had been together six months, and already seemed to have killed whatever following they might have developed by playing every week at the same dank, sticky-floored dive on the far north side.

"Make your shows more of an event," Kate told Holly. "Get a buzz going, build up your web presence."

"We're still pulling things together," Holly protested. "We're finding our sound."

"You could still be getting out there and, you know, networking."

"Networking," Holly said, putting the word in air quotes.

"Christ, I don't know, meet people, meet other bands, play somewhere other than this shithole for a change." Kate truly wanted her friend to succeed, but in her impatience with Holly's perfectionism and chronic delaying, she also felt her support curdling into control and, at times, envy. When Kate saw Holly close her eyes onstage and lose herself completely in song, a shudder went through her, and she despaired that nothing, not work, family, or even sex, could ever exert such a tidal sway over her own life.

Still, the nights when Holly Perry and the Cold, Cold Hearts played just for her (and the bored bartender who watched the Bulls on mute on the TV) felt so private that Kate found herself glaring, shushing, and finally shouting, "Shut the fuck up!" when some group of drunken idiots wandered in, listened to a few songs, then proceeded to fire up the air hockey table in the back corner and ding-ding-ding and high-five their way through the rest of the set. The repetition of the songs week after week—hearing Holly gradually strip away every unnecessary ornament, change the phrasing, change even the lyrics—made her forget exactly how the originals went. She'd come to this music through Holly, and she loved how Holly was now making these songs her own.

Toward the end of the night, when the air hockey all-stars had retired and the lonely, late-night regulars drifted in for last call, there were shots, there were fifth and sixth beers, Holly and the band playing loose and a little wild, and Kate taking swings around the floor with Lawrence, an old barfly who drank brandy old-fashioneds, smelled of CornNuts, and danced the most gentlemanly lead she'd ever encountered. There was packing up the equipment in the softly falling snow, one last shot of Jim Beam before the girls set off in Kate's Jetta. After the high of performing, Holly was often edgy and disappointed; playing to a practically empty room took its toll. On those nights, Kate would slip Dolly Parton into the CD player, and the two of them would yowl along to "Jolene," the first song Holly ever learned on guitar, as the car crunched over the fresh snow on Ashland Avenue. At home, they stayed up drinking and laughing and watching the 3 A.M. dating shows, waking the next morning to hangovers, a big greasy breakfast, and lying around in pajamas until Holly had to go to work. For Kate, the days were long, bright, and lazy. She filled what she needed to with nineteenth-century novels, trashy TV, researching law schools, and LSAT practice tests; the effortless, or almost effortless, routine of friendship took care of all the rest.

They met during high school, though they went to different schools. Regional Honors Choir brought them together. They stood next to each other in the altos; Kate couldn't stop giggling as Holly—crooked teeth, hair dyed black with skunk streaks bleached white, whispering and passing notes—tore apart the girls who preened for the director, jockeying to be chosen for the solos. Even when Kate herself won a soloist award for "Wind Beneath My Wings" at Singabration in Orlando their sophomore year, Holly seemed to consider her the one salvageable case among the rich kids from Grosse Pointe Farms.

Kate's parents tolerated her new friend, barely. Her two older brothers had set off toward the opposite shores of stern insurance-adjuster responsibility and prolonged surf-bum dissolution, leaving Kate marooned somewhere in between. The first few times she brought Holly home, her parents acted like she was staging some copycat rebellion, so she obliged them and started hanging out at Holly's house in Pontiac after school, on weekends, and all summer. Holly's mom was cool. She didn't give a rat's ass if the girls smoked cigarettes or pot in the house. Sometimes she even got high with them. Holly's mom had a beat-up Silvertone guitar, bought from a Sears catalog, that she used to play to pass the time and calm her nerves back when little baby Holly bawled her head off all day and all night. When they got truly baked, Holly and her mom traded the guitar back and forth, and the three of them, Kate included, harmonized together, singing Waylon, Hank, and Dolly. On the chorus of "Jolene" (Jolene, Jo-lene, Jo-*lene*, Jo-*leeeene*), they outdid each other with their vocal histrionics.

Then Holly's mom got laid off from Firestone, and things got grim. Because she needed help with the rent, Holly's mom let her boyfriend move in. He dealt weed and pills out of the house, and it both scared and thrilled Kate to see the kinds of people who came around. Holly was forever cussing the boyfriend out for not keeping his business separate from their lives, but he just gave her a wolfie grin and said, "Baby's gotta eat," or something stupid like that. Eventually, it became apparent that Holly's mom had gotten hooked on OxyContin, which meant she took the boyfriend's side in things as often as she took Holly's. Kate was proud of Holly for the way she stuck up for herself; the girl didn't take shit from anyone. Then one day Holly turned up on Kate's doorstep with a black eye and bruises coming up all over. At first it looked like the boyfriend's doing. But, no, Holly and her mom had come to blows after Holly flushed a bottle of pills down the crapper.

College brought a reprieve. The girls both enrolled at the University of Michigan, where Kate hedged her bets, majoring in English to indulge an infatuation with Dickens and Austen, and taking prelaw courses to placate her parents. Two years in, Holly dropped out, forsaking Pell grants and a partial scholarship to concentrate on her music. She played coffee shops, basement parties, and open mics, and improved on guitar quickly. But she sang so softly no one could hear, and after fifteen minutes, everyone was talking over the music. Kate offered to sing harmony — she loved the idea of coming in high and sweet behind Holly, giving the music some warmth and body — but Holly was less enthusiastic about it. She said she just wasn't hearing another voice in her sound.

"Written in a crappy basement, refined at a crappy bar," Perry *has said of these songs, and, indeed, there's something fugitive about this music that picks up only what it can use and discards the rest. Sparse opener "Leaving," all whispered vocals and silvery fingerpicking, sets a sepulchral tone. "Grown out of you / Walked right out on you," Perry intones on the chorus. "Miracle Mile," which takes its title from Pontiac's mile-long truck plant, is similarly stark, its desolate imagery and simple two-chord structure an icy rebuke to the hubris of bygone eras.*

Chicago was five hours from home but a world away. Or at least the neighborhood where Holly wanted to live was. All the coolest venues were there, she told Kate, all the loft spaces and artists' warehouses, all the hippest bars. After Kate's graduation, they packed up her Jetta and made the move. As they pulled away, the sight of Holly's mom crying in front of the house in Pontiac, with its shingles hanging loose and its half-dead lawn, made Kate's gut hurt. Holly just waved good-bye and didn't look back.

In Chicago, the girls found a garden apartment—exposed pipes, linoleum floors, a boiler that knocked through the night—that they could both afford. Kate's parents footed her half of the rent, giving her a year to get ready for "real life"; Holly waited tables. But the coolest clubs were booked solid, no openings for new acts without a following, and they could never seem to find these mythic lofts and warehouses where all the artists were hanging out.

Kate came home one afternoon from studying for the LSAT and heard Holly singing. She paused in the entryway, one shoe on, one shoe off. That voice—from high in the chest, not from the belly as they'd been taught in Honors Choir—always caught something in her. There was a snarl in Holly's voice, something untamed and even dissonant, an undertow of weariness, a barb of spite.

She leaned in Holly's doorway. "Is that new? Who's it by?"

"Just something I've been messing around with."

"You're writing? That's great!" Holly hadn't told her she was working on originals. She felt wounded, but she covered with bluster. "Well, come on, play it for me!"

It was a simple song in a minor key. It didn't really sound like country, and it wasn't quite folk or blues either. The flesh on that old music was meager enough; Holly had scoured it down to clean, white bones. Her fingers slipped up and down the frets, making a faint buzz as she changed chords, and she sang:

> Waking up to blank bright mornings
> Just headaches, no work, no pay
> Can't say I'm real sorry
> This life keeps slipping away

In her chest, Kate felt a trill of panic and excitement, like when she used to overhear Holly fighting with her mom. God, she could only dream of cussing out her own mother. The title of the song came in the chorus — "Don't ask 'cause I'm fine / All I need is all I got / These little blue pills and wine" — the heat in the lyrics nearly snuffed out by the coldness of the music, but still flaming up around the edges, refusing to die.

Holly played the last chord and let it ring out. Kate had to wait a minute before her tongue could unstick from her dry mouth. "Hol, it's beautiful," she said and meant it. "Are you going to show it to Billy and Patrick? Are you going to play it at the bar?"

Holly seemed not to hear. She could go away like this, slip off to some private chamber in her mind, in a way she'd never done in school, when she was all bitterness, sarcasm, and open warfare with the world. Come on, Hol, Kate sometimes wanted to say, you don't have to put on an act with me.

"I don't know if I'll show the guys," Holly finally said. "I really don't know."

———

Holly met her band through a craigslist post. Billy and Patrick were both in their early thirties, former hard-core rockers who'd gone soft and started dudding up in Western wear and growing out their beards. Patrick spent set breaks bullshitting with the bartender, trying to cadge free shots; Billy was a flirt. He was always sidling up to Kate, saying, "Hey, it's our number one fan."

"Better believe it. Number one with a bullet." She wasn't interested in him, but she returned the flirtation. Maybe because the only guys she met—her LSAT study group, Jesus, not many prospects there—were always trying to drag her out to sports bars and Bulls games. Maybe because Billy believed in Holly so deeply, or anyway he was constantly talking up Holly's talent: "She's so raw, you know? Everything she sings, she *feels*." He was already orchestrating their future musical conquests: the record they would make together, the famous bands ("huge, but not too huge") they'd open for, their first tour as a headliner, and subsequent collaborations with their musical idols.

"Number one with a bullet," Billy said. "Know where that comes from? Billboard used to put bullets next to singles that sold a million copies. It said, Look, this thing is blowing up! Not that anyone gives a shit about Billboard anymore," he quickly added.

When Billy landed the band their first big gig—a spot in the Twang Off, a battle of the bands for local country acts—he went around practically crowing.

The next week at the bar, a drummer showed up to play with the band. "Kate," Billy said proudly, "meet Tim. He's a professional jazz musician." The drummer was tall, broad-shouldered, serious-looking, a little sullen. She was immediately attracted to him.

"Well, a *professional*, pleased to meet you."

"We've met before, right?" the drummer said distractedly.

"I would've remembered you." She gave the "you" another coy little stress.

"Feel like I've seen you around," he said, shrugging. For fuck's sake, why couldn't guys ever tell when she was hitting on them? The drummer turned back to Billy.

"So, you're getting paid for this gig, right?"

The room was packed. Kate scanned the crowd: girls in Frye boots and Doris Day dresses; boys in seed jackets, seed caps, and vintage Wranglers. Scenesters: they dressed like anyone but themselves.

She found Holly, waved her over to the bar, and bought them both shots. "You'll be great," Kate said, "don't worry." She hesitated, then added, "This is kind of a party crowd, but just don't think about it."

Holly gave her a hurt look, and she instantly regretted saying it. But hadn't she been there for Holly in all those Ann Arbor coffee shops, all those Tuesday nights at the dive on the north side? Wasn't it her right, her responsibility even, to try to cushion her against failure?

Onstage, Holly seemed nervous. She didn't acknowledge the crowd, only bowed her head and tuned her guitar. Fear put a tremolo in her voice for the first verse of "You Ain't Goin' Nowhere," but by the time the chorus came around, she was amazing. It was the first time she'd sung with a full band through a good sound system, and Kate was stunned, hearing her so clearly, how far her friend had come in six months.

Patrick and Tim were solid and unobtrusive. Billy, on the other hand, fell to pieces. On "Your Cheatin' Heart," he played in the wrong key. In the second chorus of "Amanda," he messed up the melody line. And when he took up his musical saw for "Orphan Girl," he cut himself, and someone had to run and get toilet paper and a Band-Aid. He was ready to soldier on and play the last song, but Holly waved him off. "I'm gonna give the boys a little break," she said, handling it beautifully, Kate thought, "and play y'all a new one." And then Holly sang "Little Blue Pills and Wine."

The whole room went still. People quit talking. It was almost too much to take: Kate saw the house in Pontiac again, the blinds drawn, candy wrappers and beer cans all over the coffee table, Holly's mom nodding out on the couch. She felt the cold at the windows, saw the empty streets and boarded-up houses. She saw the photos of Holly's dad, who split when Holly was born, hidden away in drawers, and the old guitar with its broken strings stashed somewhere out of sight. Holly let the last chord ring out. Slowly, the crowd woke up. A few people clapped loudly. Others seemed confused—Kate had been right, this was a party crowd. But it didn't matter what anyone else thought. When Holly made it back to the bar, Kate gave her a long, fierce hug. "That was amazing," she said, unable to put what she felt into any other words. And Holly, too, seemed overwhelmed by what had just happened.

They didn't have long to revel in the feeling. The next band was already starting. The singer wore jean shorts and a rag of a T-shirt. He had a disheveled Prince Valiant haircut and a tattoo of two snakes twining the neck of an electric guitar down the length of his arm. "I like to twang off every night before bed," he drawled into the microphone, and then shouted out "1-2-3-4!" The band was called the Pickup Fucks, and they drowned out the memory of Holly's set with sheer volume. The crowd went wild. After a couple songs even Holly was bopping along. Across the room Billy stood aghast; the battle was lost. Except for dirty Prince Valiant, the Pickup Fucks all had bushy wildman beards. They put Billy's and Patrick's beards to shame.

After these blasts of north wind, Perry tries to warm things up a little. "Killed in a Song," a Cash-Carter-style duet with Kitt Daniels, Perry's sometime boyfriend, finds her in sultry, stoned-out mode. But the title track, a halfhearted (forgive the pun) attempt at revved up honky-tonk, is a misstep. Perry sounds best when wounded and detached. Joy and human connection—not her strong suit.

Billy managed to get the band a few slots opening for local groups, ones Kate had never heard of but were supposedly "established." And more people were showing up to the dive on the far north side every week. Both Holly and the Cold, Cold Hearts seemed to be gaining confidence, and Billy had the foresight to have the teeth on his saw filed down. The new drummer only showed half the time (paying gigs took precedence), but when he did, the music took on a heft it never had before. It was like seeing a real act—the sets had shape and drama. Kate watched people's eyes light up when Holly covered "Jolene." She overheard a girl say to her friend, "Oh my God, that's my favorite Loretta Lynn song!" As for old Lawrence, he'd never known such a wealth of dance partners.

Holly started playing more of her originals. The band approached this new material tentatively, unsure how to embellish such skeletal structures. The audience, too, was slow to warm to these unfamiliar songs, and only Kate had the thrill of recognition when Holly picked out the first notes of "Miracle Mile" or "U.P. Blues."

The LSAT was approaching, too quickly. Kate's study group was meeting three times a week, and one night she let the others talk her into going to a bar called Sluggers, where she drank too many Long Island Ice Teas and got sucked into their chatter about admissions stats and padding out applications. She came home sloshed and merry and heard Holly playing guitar and singing. She was about to burst into Holly's room and sprawl out on the bed when another voice stopped her cold. It was reedy, drawling, somehow perverse. Holly made an adjustment in pitch, and she and the drawling voice locked into tight harmony. Kate retreated to the living room, put the TV on, turned up the volume. Forty minutes later, the visitor came out, slouching on a leather jacket, ruffling his greasy helmet of hair, mumbling a slurred "Hey, what's up?" in Kate's direction, and then exiting the building. Holly came out of her room, grinning about something.

"Oh, please don't tell me you made out with him!" Kate said. "He's so gross!"

"Really?" Holly said. "I think he's hot."

"He's so fake. I can't stand the fake poor thing, the ripped clothes and all that."

Holly raised an eyebrow at this but said only, "He's been helping me out with some things."

"Like what?"

"I don't know"—Holly yawned happily, like a kitten lying in sunshine—"getting better gigs, song craft."

"*Song craft*? His music sucks. It's just shouting."

"I dig his band. They nail the whole cow-punk thing. Anyway, why are you so pissed off? I haven't gotten some in forever."

"Well, neither have I."

"Then try being happy for me," Holly said, slumping down in front of the TV and changing the channel from *Blind Date* to some Discovery Channel special about comets.

Kate spent the rest of the night in her room, stewing. She understood suddenly how lonely she was; she had no other friends in Chicago and had been investing way too much time in Holly, in trying to tend to Holly's ego. She wrapped herself in the covers and tried to plow through another practice LSAT. She'd come to take comfort in the way the tests made her slot her thinking into tidy little spaces and gave her days structure and purpose, but now the arguments and logic games kept sliding out from under her concentration. Finally, she gave up and called her mother in Grosse Pointe. She kept trying to unload; she was boiling over; she was going to scream. But her mother had her own complaints: the contractors redoing the veranda were taking really far too long, the city was out there tearing up the road again, and with all the hammering she'd been getting these awful headaches—God, sometimes her skull felt like it was about to split.

Holly got a job bartending at Rainbo Club, a bar they'd always passed over for being too trendy. One of Kitt's friends was the manager, of course. Between band practice and work, Holly was hardly home. She opened for the Pickup Fucks for a string of gigs. Holly's drummer went off on tour with some radio-rock band, and the guy from Kitt's band started filling in. Nearly a month went by, and Kate skipped all of Holly's performances. If she didn't buckle down now, she told herself, she'd never get into a first-tier school. But apathy descended. She'd always thought she would neatly sidestep her parents' expectations by disappearing into the penurious obscurity of labor law or public defense. She knew what it was like out there, how hard it was for ordinary people. But given what her study group had been saying, even if you did sell out, you weren't going to be strolling right into a job. Not these days. You had to get a foot in the door, and early. Was she really so ready to consign herself to three years of misery, nothing but homework and sucking up to professors, with no guarantee at the end? What was so wrong with being secure? U of M, Northwestern Law, junior partner by thirty-five—it was what her father had wanted from all three of his children. She'd always trusted his judgment, always wanted to be worthy of him. Holly disapproved, naturally, and thought she should wait out her ambivalence, figure out what she really loved. But where would Holly be in ten years? Twenty? Hardly anyone made a living playing music; you practically had to give yourself away. What was wrong with thinking your time was actually *worth* something?

—————

She went to see Holly play at the Hideout. It was supposed to be some big-deal venue, "a launching pad," as Kitt put it. At the door, she gave her name for the guest list, but Holly hadn't put her on. She was about to pay the cover, but then, in a fit of pique, turned around and went home.

Holly got back late that night. She kicked off her boots in the middle of the living room and flopped down on the couch, toppling a pile of Kate's flashcards.

"Hey, you missed a great night! We were *on*. Such a great vibe!"

"You didn't put me on the list."

"Oh, shit, sorry. I wasn't sure you'd come, and then Kitt said this blogger was going to check out the bill and to put him on. But he didn't show. Sorry, I was going to text you." She took her weed from the end-table drawer and started packing a bowl. "I'm still amped up. Want to get high?"

"I have to study," Kate said coldly. She got up to go to her room, and tripped over Holly's boots. It was an excuse, though she felt she didn't need one, to pick a fight.

First she scolded Holly for never cleaning up after herself, never doing the dishes, leaving her shit everywhere. And all that time she spent practicing—didn't she think anyone else might like a little quiet now and then? All Holly seemed to care about was her music, about "making it." (Here, Kate mimicked the acid tone Holly had taken when they'd talked about networking.) Kate felt abandoned. She'd been loyal, absolutely loyal to Holly, and she'd been abandoned. "We don't talk anymore," Kate said, which for her was the ultimate sign of betrayal, but also now an invitation for Holly to apologize.

Of course Holly, when cornered, wasn't much for apologizing.

She was tired, she said—sighing to show just how tired she was—of Kate treating her like a little sister, of always having to listen to her goddamn advice about everything.

"You'd never do anything if no one pushed you," Kate shot back, feeling both appalled at herself and excited, almost giddy, as she said it. She felt like she was going to break out laughing. "I mean, you've been surrounded by fuck-ups your whole life, and now, surprise, it's all Kitt, Kitt, Kitt."

"You don't know a thing about him."

"Oh, he looks great right now," Kate went on, "all drunk and dangerous. That worked out real nice for your mom, didn't it? Some track record. I'm just surprised you didn't start ruining yourself sooner."

"Wow," Holly said, feigning a gasp. "Wow. Good thing I've had you looking out for me. Thank you so much for stooping so low to hang out with *trash* all these years. Fucking tourist," Holly muttered, "quit sucking off my life."

Kate tried to keep up her end of the fight, but the wind had gone out of her. She took another tack: She was sick of living in Holly's dirty world, dirty bars and dirty people with their Goodwill clothes and their bullshit pretentiousness. They thought they mattered so much, when they didn't matter at all. While other people went out and ran the world and made a difference, Kitt and his buddies just hung around practically sucking each other's dicks. She was sick to death of them. Sick to death of living in this shitty neighborhood and this shitty apartment and doing nothing but getting high and listening to bands no one would care about in a year anyway.

And then to prove what kind of a rage she was in, Kate picked up the boot she'd tripped over and hurled it against the wall. Holly had seen much worse than this little display and stood there smirking, unimpressed. Kate stomped off to her room. A few minutes later, she heard Holly go out the front door, slamming it behind her.

The two of them had fought before and always made up. But this fight seemed somehow necessary and sickeningly final. Kate kept waiting for things to snap back to normal. Holly of all people should understand her need to release some frustration and anger. But Holly acted like she didn't have the time to make up. She was always at Kitt's or working late, and the few times she came home, she went straight to her room and didn't make a sound, as if chiding Kate for raising a stink over her practicing guitar.

Kate was so desperate for company that one night she took down Holly's phone list and called Tim, the professional drummer, out of the blue and asked him on a date. He was gigging every night of the week, so they met for afternoon coffee in Wicker Park. She had a better time than she thought she would. He was funny and gave her lots of compliments, and though he talked too much about all the bands he was gigging with, he only mentioned Holly in passing.

"Do you ever play to no one?" she asked him. "Like a completely empty room. Doesn't it hurt when that happens?"

He laughed. Even his laugh was vaguely mournful. "A real musician doesn't need to care what anyone else thinks. That's something you learn early: Be self-sufficient." He was about to go on when Kate burst into tears. She blubbered and swiped at her nose with her sleeve, and people started turning to look; she was sure this cute guy was going to run out the door. He sat there looking panicked, then uncomfortable, then concerned. Finally, he took her hand and pulled her out into the bright May sunshine, and they walked up Milwaukee Avenue till she'd gotten herself together. He even knew not to ask what was wrong.

Kitt Daniels' band, Chicago stalwarts the Pickup Fucks, provides sensitive, sympathetic accompaniment throughout—no surprise given the months they spent backing Perry on tour. The last third of the album, an exquisitely vulnerable acoustic affair recorded dry and close, harks back to Perry's early days playing coffeehouses solo. If Heart of Hearts *accomplishes nothing else, it is a much-needed corrective to the chest-beating rock and hip-hop that came out of the Motor City in the 90s. In Perry's world, the car always breaks down, they shut the power off at the worst time, and the regrets pile up as fast as the bills.*

There was a phone call. It came on the landline. The voice on the other end asked for Holly, and for a moment Kate thought it was someone from a record company and she thrilled to think she might be the one to break the news. Then she recognized the voice: the boyfriend—calling to say the house in Pontiac had burned down.

When Kate got hold of Holly, she seemed unsurprised. "The fucker was probably cooking meth or something. I guess I'll have to go up there now."

"Why don't you take Kitt with you?" Kate tried to make it sound like an honest suggestion and not recrimination.

"He's playing this weekend."

Neither of them spoke. Finally, Kate said, "I can take you up there. I haven't been home in a while anyway."

"You don't have to do that," Holly said, and then, "Thanks."

Kate canceled her plans with Tim for the weekend and told her study group she'd catch up on the material. They left that Friday, driving most of the way in a mutually stubborn silence, only softening a little when an oldies station they used to listen to started coming in. Holly asked what she wanted to do with the apartment. She figured since she was at Kitt's most of the time it made sense for her to get off the lease. Kate told a half-truth: "I've been looking at places in Lincoln Park." She wanted to move there, but she hadn't been looking. She waited for Holly to say something caustic. Lincoln Park: Yuppies, rich singles, Cubs fans.

"It'll be an easy commute if you get in to Northwestern."

Kate felt sick to her stomach. She couldn't bear this business-like conversation. "I'd better ace the damn LSAT first. Two weeks to go." The Dolly Parton CD was in the glove box. Why couldn't they just put it in, sing along, pretend nothing had happened?

"Two weeks," Holly said. "Break a leg."

On the way to the hotel where Holly's mom and the boyfriend were staying, they stopped to see the damage. The house had been scorched out like a jack-o'-lantern, but not burned to the ground. Part of the roof had collapsed. Otherwise, the house didn't look much worse than the vacant, foreclosed homes surrounding it. They got out of the car and stood in the lightly falling spring rain. Holly ducked under the yellow cordon tape and put her key in the lock. They went inside.

Ash like thick dust lay over everything, burn marks made weird patterns on the ceiling, and the shag carpet was spotted with black circles, as if marking the spots where they'd once sat cross-legged with Holly's mom, smoking dope and singing old songs. In the center of the living room a space heater had been reduced to a droopy chunk of plastic. Holly kicked it over. "How much you want to bet they were huddling around this piece of shit?"

Kate asked was she doing okay. In the hallway, Holly tugged open the closet and started digging through it. "Hol, you sure you're okay?"

"Where is it?" A stack of boxes collapsed, and Holly screamed, "Where the *fuck* is it?" Kate found her friend in her arms. "Goddamn it." Holly was shaking, trying to catch her breath. "Goddamn it, I wanted that guitar. It was supposed to be mine."

Kate stood smoothing her friend's hair, saying, "It's all right, don't worry, it'll be okay." She'd wanted this for long time, she knew. Even before their fight, she'd secretly wished for a disaster that would bring her and Holly back together, back to the way they'd been when they were girls. Now the calamity had arrived, she was disgusted with herself for calling it down.

Then she saw the dusty black case sticking out between some boxes.

"Hol, look."

The old Sears catalog guitar had escaped, both fire and pawnshop. Holly twanged a string. The note rang out through the still house. Kate waited, waited for Holly to look up at her, just one look of acknowledgment to say this beat-up guitar meant something for both of them. But Holly was lost in inspecting the thing, testing the strings for life, winding the tuners, checking to see the neck wasn't warped. And when she did look up, her face was inscrutable: too many of her own memories roiling behind it.

They drove over to the hotel, a cheap place with both *a*'s missing in Vacancy.

"Want me to come in?" Kate said, though she knew what Holly's answer would be.

"I'll be okay. I've been putting up with their shit long enough."

They sat in silence. This was the moment for reconciliation, for either of them to apologize. They hugged, quick and hard. Holly got out of the car, carrying her suitcase and the guitar like someone about to get on a Greyhound bus and go far away. Kate pulled out of the lot and headed for Grosse Pointe and home, driving through Holly's neighborhood again. She watched the signs pass by and read them aloud to herself—Stella's Chicken and Donut, Cracked Windshield Repair Here, Cash for Your Olde Gold—as if to commit them to memory.

Closing track "Silvertone," a waltz-time lament for a departed lover, is a lapse into sentimentality, a studio outtake that a more mature artist would surely have left off the record. Still, there's something thrilling about hearing Perry completely unguarded. You can feel the nerves, the fragility. As the tape begins to roll, Perry fumbles with her guitar, unsure what comes next.

Holly played a loft party in Pilsen. Kitt had organized it as a showcase for her. The crowd was older, mostly men in their thirties with thinning hair, dressed in sport coats over faded band T-shirts. Half of them wore mustaches—beards were out—and all the freshly shaven cheeks looked fishy white and vulnerable. When Kitt saw Kate come in, he waved her over. She pushed her way across the room. "This place is packed," she said when she got to Kitt. She never knew what to say to him.

"Pitchfork people," he explained. "Once they hear about an act breaking, they come *en masse*."

"Are you singing tonight?"

"I might get up for a couple. Just a couple. It's Hol's night."

Hol. Everyone had started calling her that lately.

"This is great. I like this space. It's packed," she said again.

Next to the donations table, there was a tub of beer on ice. There was a lighter on the table, and she made a fumbling attempt at using it to open a bottle. "Here," Kitt said, taking the lighter, and in one practiced motion, popping the cap. Foam came rushing up the neck, spilling over them both. Kitt brushed his hair out of his eyes and grinned at her. In that moment, Kate had to admit it—he was sexy.

The rest of the Pickup Fucks were setting up their equipment. Kate went over and found Holly next to the stage, winding a string onto her Sears guitar.

"Where are the Cold, Cold Hearts?" It occurred to her that, with everything else going on, she hadn't seen Billy or Patrick for weeks.

"I thought it'd just be easier to play with Kitt's guys," Holly said. "Tonight's kind of a big deal, and . . . well, you've seen Billy."

This news made Kate sad, but she tried to not to show it.

Holly started changing the next string. "Shit," she said, glancing up at Kate, "I'm really fucking nervous for this thing."

Don't think about it, Kate started to say, then stopped herself. Holly was only giving her a chance to go through their old ceremony. She didn't need pep talks anymore.

The lights dipped, and then Kitt was at the microphone, welcoming everyone, introducing the band. "You'll be great!" Kate called out—she couldn't help it. Holly said something, but over the noise, Kate didn't hear. She gave Holly a little wave and worked her way through the crowd till she found a spot near the back. Holly climbed onstage, adjusted her microphone, then turned her back to the audience to tune her guitar.

Just then, Kate felt a presence behind her. Someone touched her shoulder.

"I'm pumped for this show, aren't you?" He had curly blond hair and wore blue-framed glasses and a blue T-shirt matching them. He introduced himself, but his name went right out of her head. He told her he wrote about music for a Web site. "We're kind of tastemakers," he explained. "We're known for that."

"Oh," Kate said, trying to be polite for Holly's sake, "that's cool."

"I saw you guys talking before the show." He gestured toward the stage. "You know her?"

"We grew up together."

The boy raised his eyebrows. "What was *that* like?"

"What was what like?"

"I mean, it must have been hard on you both, growing up there."

"Well, I'm not really from Pontiac. I guess it's pretty rough, but—"

"Yeah, totally. That's what her songs are about, right? About the devastation the boom and bust economy wreaks on the working class? About the way people survive." He looked at Holly as he talked. "But there's still a pop sensibility there. I mean that song 'Reckon Up,' that could totally be a hit. But I respect how she always hews off toward something more fractured, something more austere. Do you think you could introduce me?" he said suddenly. "After the show, I'd love to talk to her."

She was about to answer, to say yes, when the crowd hushed. Holly stepped up to the mic.

"Is it rolling?" you can just hear her whisper to herself. "Is it rolling?"

Sidemen

The young salesman has been flirting from the moment I came through the door. He's spaghetti pale and about as skinny, smiles at me like we're already intimate. His hair is done up in spectacular dirty blond dreadlocks — he plays with the end of one as he talks. We're back in the drum department, surrounded by an arsenal of instruments: cymbals, tambourines, maracas, rows and rows of drum sets. "Ma'am, what you're looking for," my young salesman says, hoisting up a wooden, hourglass-shape drum, "is this."

This music store is warehouse-sized, busier, louder, and more intimidating than the fleabag places August dragged me into before he began his perpetual tour. Clusters of longhaired boys mill around, occasionally picking up guitars and other pieces of equipment to produce various skronks and squalls.

"That looks familiar." I almost have to shout to be heard over the racket.

"It's called a *djembe*," my salesman says. "It's from Africa. Totally authentic. And check it out, the skin on top" — he kneels and pounds out a rhythm — "real animal."

He looks up at me mischievously, says, "Let's ring it up." At the register, he tries selling me on a traveling bag, a carrying strap, an instructional book, some kind of special oil to treat the skin. About the only thing he doesn't ask for is my phone number.

"It's a surprise going away gift," I finally tell him. "For graduation. My daughter, Senna."

"Oh, right on." He looks so deflated by knowing I'm a mother that I feel obliged to continue the conversation.

"So, what do you play? Drums?"

He laughs. "I'm a DJ."

"Oh, a disc jockey." I wonder if this makes him a musician or a radio personality. "What kind of music do you . . . do?"

He breaks into a grin. He's still in the boyish part of his midtwenties and all swagger. A handsome kid in his way, and doesn't he know it. He gives me a long, rehearsed answer, but it's all too hip and technical — "house" and "funk" are the only *words* I even recognize. When he finishes by telling me that he plays a club called Elevated every Wednesday, that I should come down sometime, he'll put me on the guest list, I can only offer lamely, "You know, my husband is a musician too."

My salesman walks me and the drum to the front door. "If you need anything else, Sue," he says (got my name off the credit card, clever), "call and ask for me." I look down at his nametag. It reads "Dave."

"There are five Daves here," he says, "ask for Trance. DJ Trance."

"Right on," I say, teasing him a little, though he doesn't seem to notice.

"Oh, one more thing." He slides a pad and pen from his pocket. "It's for our records. Can I have your phone number?"

I took off early from the office, hoping to miss rush hour on Lake Shore Drive, but the drive up to Rogers Park is brutal. I have the drum—the *djembe*—buckled into the passenger seat. Its skin is ringed with fur and the wood carved with designs of stickmen dancing and hunting with spears. I've never seen these drum circles Senna and her friends drive to on the south side, and as any mother would, I worry about what goes on at them. But I like the idea of Senna taking her own instrument along. And, really, drum circles seem pretty innocent next to what August and I did in our late teens.

Traffic is at a standstill. The thought of dragging myself up three flights of stairs to the apartment and finding nobody home is making the waiting both excruciating and a sort of blessing. I give the top of the drum a thump. A note booms out so deep and resonant the rearview mirror shakes.

When I get home and get the drum hidden in my closet, I find a note from Senna. *With Cindy. Conga Beach. Back 8 pm? 9 pm??* It isn't even signed.

Seeing it . . . I've had some bad evenings lately, but this one . . . I don't know, suddenly I'm overcome. There are no new messages on the answering machine, no calls from August. The dishes in the drying rack tell me Senna was home and made herself an early dinner. Cooking is one of the few things that keep me distracted these days; I'm almost angry at Senna for feeding herself. When I open the cupboard, all I find is a box of brownie mix from, well, it must be years ago because it's not organic but merely "all natural." This gives me an idea I already know is a bad one.

Even though he hid it (he hid it!) last time he was home from tour, I still find August's stash quickly enough. It's stuffed in the sound hole of his prized Martin acoustic guitar, looking very stale after three months sitting there unsmoked. Half an hour later, I'm sliding a hot pan of brownies out of the oven. Standing there, holding it between oven mitts, I say aloud to no one, "Throw it away. You pathetic woman, throw it away."

Instead, I cut myself a generous piece, take it into the living room, and kneel in front of August's hi-fi. One of Senna's CDs is sitting on top of the player. I put it in, press play, and move myself and my brownie to the couch.

The first bite is awful, even worse than I remember laced brownies tasting. And though I would love to surprise Senna sometime with my deep appreciation for her music, the badly tuned guitars and vague, wandering melodies miss my auditory synapses by a few generations, even with the buzz from the brownie creeping up. I change Senna's CD for Neil Young, *After the Goldrush*, which at least matches my mood—maudlin, nostalgic, reasonably reckless. . . .

The dead bolt on the front door clunking open wakes me. First thing I see is the record still spinning on the turntable, then the digits on the VCR clock come into focus. Eleven P.M. I hear Senna kicking off her shoes in the hallway. When I stand, I realize I'm still high.

I get myself to the kitchen counter and seize the bake pan. My first thought, a thought that feels like a holdover from ten years ago, is, Hey, calm down, Mom. Why not just offer Senna some? My second thought: I am not *that* sort of mother. Christ, if I ever become that mother, I'll—

"Sorry I'm late," Senna calls out, "We went back to Cindy's to play Scrabble."

I throw open the back door, rattle down the fire escape, and pitch the brownies, bake pan and all, into the dumpster behind the building. "Hey," Senna says when I get back up, "what are you doing?"

"Mouse," I say. "A big one. I trapped it."

"Damn," Senna says as she puts on the kettle for a cup of tea, her nightly ritual, "you let it go, right?" She's wearing her favorite white peasant dress, has her blond hair in a braid, and smells of cigarettes. She is not some tiny, delicate thing, and while I have worried that it hurts her to know this, the presence she brings to a room is irrepressible. She's been experimenting, since age thirteen, with piercings and dyeing her hair, but tonight she is unadorned and radiant. When the track lighting catches a thin line of hair above her lip, I'm almost proud to see it's been months since she last waxed.

I prop myself against the kitchen island. Standing fully on my own power, pretending I'm not stoned, and holding a conversation with my daughter at the same time is feeling near impossible. AP History paper? *Got an A-, but going to revise and turn in again.* Cindy? *Is good.* Conga Beach? *Fun.* Who was there? *Cindy, Justin, Stephen, Shane, Mark K., Mark T., Marco.* Who's . . . Mark K? *You remember, Mark T.'s friend, from Orland Park, he broke his arm jet-skiing but he wouldn't wear a cast and . . .*

When I'm down to leaning on my elbows just to stay vertical, Senna fixes me with a curious look. "Everything okay, Mom?"

"A little sick. The air quality today."

"Hey," she says, "some kids at school were asking about getting their copies of the new album signed. Think Dad would mind?"

No, he wouldn't. Getting them to him, wherever he is, is the problem. "We'll ask Rick," I woozily tell her.

Then I excuse myself off to bed, where I quietly vomit in my wastebasket, pass out on top of the sheets, and dream vivid dreams about I don't remember what.

Work the next day . . . less than stellar.

You know, my husband is a musician. A famous musician, actually. "The August Rawling Band," says the most recent *Sun-Times* clipping stuck to my fridge with a pickle magnet, "began with a chance meeting that is quickly becoming the stuff of legend. In '77, Rawling spent six months in Cook County on charges that he conspired to raid, and allegedly burn down, the offices of Mayor Richard J. Daley. In County, Rawling met the notorious local drug peddler, poet, and musician Wildcat John Jackson, who, with a contraband guitar smuggled into the prison, taught Rawling the songs of Woody Guthrie, Howlin' Wolf, Phil Ochs, and Big Bill Broonzy." (This is only part true. August met John several times, but he learned all those songs off his mom's old LPs.)

"Rawling describes the songs he wrote after his imprisonment as 'full of rage, but still flailing about in the straitjacket of the system.' Twenty years later, the rage remains, but Rawling has found the venues for his activism. 'We'll play in front of 20,000 people one night,' Rawling says, 'and then do rallies or fund-raisers for 200 the next three. If I'm broke by the time the August Rawling Band plays its last note, I'll be happy.'"

My husband says nearly the same thing in the scores of articles written on this new album. *CMJ*, *Spin*, *NME*, the *Reader*, the *Nation*. Even *Newsweek* ran a little sidebar. They all go on to mention his "tough-times upbringing on Chicago's west side," the influence of his socialist parents (who named him after August Spies, of Haymarket infamy), and, of course, his near constant touring. All of it straight out of the press kit—August is as interested in making his myth as they are in propagating it. My favorite encomium from *Rolling Stone*: "The songs on *Truck Stops and Troubadours* are clear-eyed without being defeated. Rawling's almost evangelical activist nature has been leavened by a new sense of road-worn wisdom."

What the reviews don't mention is the wife August met when they were both seventeen, who would've been along for the Daley sit-in if she hadn't been pregnant, who bore him a daughter when he was off playing a rally; the wife who got realistic (or maybe just tired) and gave up nonprofit for a nine-to-five in PR; the wife who thought a "creative" career might still give her time for her painting and photography; the wife who actually likes having a decent, stable income; the wife who eats stale pot brownies at home alone and obsesses over the safety of their daughter.

In the article stuck to my fridge there's a photo of August cradling his guitar. Despite the nose that got itself broken in two places by a cop and the male-pattern baldness tied back into a ponytail, August is photogenic. "Rawling's electric live performances," the caption reads, "which he often does for free or for charity, attract hard-core utopian commies and tuned-in teenage girls alike."

My trouble: Whenever I read that caption, I go a deeply flattered shade of scarlet. I am the original girl in the audience, now inching cautiously through her early forties, wondering how much those hippie girls in halter tops would envy her if they knew the rest of the story.

Thursday night our friends come over for a drink—Saul, works for the record label that signed August; Rick, his manager; and Evie, Rick's partner of the last seven months. Our friends: August's friends.

"We hit three hundred thousand copies this morning," Rick says before they even get through the door. He pulls a bottle of champagne out of a brown paper bag and pops the top right there in the hallway. "Kudos all around. Let's drink this stuff up."

I'm not sure if he's congratulating me or Saul, but I certainly didn't have much to do with the thing. Last time August was home, he was in the studio three weeks straight putting the finishing touches on. I think they added mandolin to one song and took it off another. Senna and I didn't see much of him. He took her down to the studio a couple of times, but she said it was boring. I found that out a long time ago.

We sit down in the front room. "All right, guys," I say. "All right already. I call a moratorium on band talk."

Evie takes my hand sympathetically. She's thirty-eight and beautiful in that tanning-bed sort of way. "All of this must make you wonder why you married the man in the first place," she says laughingly. Rick used to have such good taste in girlfriends.

"Been down this road before," I mutter. Eight albums, eight tours. I'm an old hand.

"But this one's selling like crazy," Saul says.

"Moratorium!" I protest. "Moratorium!"

"Come on, Susie," Rick says. "Let us get a little excited for you guys."

"No band talk. Let me show you what I got Senna for her graduation."

I go into the bedroom, pull the *djembe* out of the closet, hug it awkwardly to my chest. It's heavier than I remember. Waddling like a duck, I bring it into the front room.

"*In the deepest, darkest Congo,*" Rick says in a hushed voice, taking the drum from me, "*we heard the ever-constant beating of the tom-toms.*" He leans over and pounds out a wild rhythm. The champagne glasses on the coffee table clink and rattle. Do all men feel the need to beat a drum when presented one?

"What a brute," Evie says.

"*Djembe,*" I say. "It's called a *djembe.*"

We finish the champagne, and I get a couple of bottles of white from the fridge. Despite me, it's beginning to feel like a celebration.

Evie turns to me. "So, where's Senna tonight? What's Senna been up to?"

I don't know. No note on the counter this afternoon, no messages on the machine, not even a whiff of cigarette smoke in the air. But I can't tell Evie this. If Evie thinks she's being bullshitted, she goes into interrogation mode, and you're under the lamps of her mascara-ed eyes for the next two hours.

"Senna," I begin, "spends every waking hour with her friends, most of whom are boys, most of whose names all sound the same to me. And they spend all their time at a park called Conga Beach, which is somewhere, don't ask me, on the south side."

Rick and Saul lean back into the couch. Both cross their legs. The room has gone suddenly quiet. What have I said?

"And why does Senna keep escaping to this beach?" Evie says.

"Because she loves these drum things. She talks about them all the time, all these people she meets. And the boys, of course. Plenty of cute boys too stoned not to be taken advantage of."

Rick and Saul laugh, but Evie is intent on her probing. "Don't cover up how you feel about Senna," she admonishes. She leans toward me, hands held out palms up as if I were about to lay a baby or a ripe watermelon in her arms. "Don't conceal yourself." This from a woman who uses more petroleum products on her face than I do in my car.

"Well, I feel like she's finding her way in the world, and that I couldn't stop her even if I tried, and that if I *did* try it'll just hurt more when she's gone."

"Kids gotta leave sometime," Saul adds in, though he's never had any of his own. "Where's she want to go to school?"

"What, college? She didn't even apply, thinks it's too easy, too obvious. Blame August for that one."

Rick and Saul chuckle in knowing agreement.

"So now it's New York, San Francisco, Portland, Vancouver, London. She keeps saying, 'What do you think, Mom? How about Beijing?' Christ, she's an ambitious kid. I mean, she interviewed Studs Terkel for a *book report*. She and Cindy are going to strap on their packs and never come back. She wants to follow her father's footsteps. No big deal, right?" I feel suddenly inflamed by this notion. My cheeks go hot, and I can't keep it from coming out. "Blame me—wife couldn't give him enough to keep him at home. If he was sleeping around you'd tell me, right? Saul? Rick?" Rick and Saul stare into their wine glasses. There's something interesting at the bottom apparently. I break into a high laugh that sounds psychotic even to me.

"It's just a bunch of smelly guys on that bus," Saul offers.

"No girls allowed," Rick intones.

Saul seems to think this an off note. "August is loyal," he says firmly. "He's committed. It ain't rock and roll, but he is."

Evie gets up and goes to the toilet. Rick and Saul sit there fidgeting. They try to ask me about work, but I'm clearly upset. Neither of them really understands what I do anyway. Evie comes back with her jacket on, ready to leave. "We'll let you get on," Rick seconds, as if I had a roast in the oven and needed to get back to basting it.

After I see them down to the front gate, I pick up the bottles and glasses, straighten the kitchen, and then burst into tears. I've always tried to think of crying as a resource, the thing that makes you feel better when everything else is used up. Tonight I decide that's the stupidest idea I've had in my life. When it's time for bed, I borrow one of Senna's tea bags and put on the kettle. The phone rings.

I half expect it to be Evie calling to lob one last spitball of wisdom my way. Instead, a male voice calling itself a police officer. I don't get the name, only hear him say the words "your daughter." I'm down on my knees, clutching the phone like a lifeline. It's like being hit with a wall of water. I'm drowning.

"What?" I manage to get out. "Sorry?"

The officer pauses to say in a slightly more tender version of his nasal accent, "Ma'am, she's just fine, okay? Her friend—Ms. Taylor—might be talking with us awhile. Ms. Rawling just needs a ride home. This *is* her mother speaking?"

"Yes," I say, "God, yes. What do I do?"

In my rush to the car, I leave the phone hanging off the hook, the back gate unlocked, and the kettle whistling a dying tune about negligent parenting.

After I interrogate the desk sergeant, I'm confident that what happened involved Cindy getting picked up for dealing some pills at the park—though one thing I've learned about cops in my time, they *never* give you enough to make the complete picture. I wait in the precinct lobby an hour before a door opens and Senna shuffles out. She's wearing a wildly improbable outfit: checkered skirt, hoop earrings, army surplus button-down.

I'm all set to start my scolding, but when we get close, I see how slack Senna's face has gone and pull her into me so hard I feel her ribs against mine. If this is my new program of tough love . . . not a good start.

On the Kennedy driving back home, Senna reaches over and takes my hand. I ask if she wants to tell me what happened. She shakes her head no. A moment later, she says in a rush, "Cindy was just trying to sell some stuff she bought at the beach a few weeks ago. She didn't want it anymore. She only wanted to . . . And then this big guy bursts out of nowhere flashing a badge, and then he's got our friend Rainy in cuffs — just because Rainy's black, Mom. I mean Rainy was just . . ." She trails away until the only sound is the skittering of highway gravel against the car's undercarriage.

"So what were they?" I ask.

"What were what?"

"Come on, the pills. Ecstasy? Uppers, downers, ludes?"

She lets go of my hand. "It was Ecstasy."

"Okay, well, Ecstasy. Senna, you have to know how dangerous those — "

"And some PCP."

"PCP!" I slow down so I can attempt to drive and glare at my daughter at the same time. "Senna, this means we're going to have a very serious talk about drugs."

She snorts. "You want to handle that one, or should Dad?"

So I wasn't fooling her in the kitchen the other night after all.

"Well, *don't* listen, then," I say. I choose to be angry now, angry in the overblown way you get when you stub your toe. "You won't have to listen to me or your father when you're gone, or follow any of our rules, so why listen now?"

"I'm not gone yet," Senna says quietly.

"No, but I wish you'd tell me exactly when you are going, so I can get on with *my* fucking life, as pathetic as you probably think it is."

"Shit, Mom . . ." She falls silent.

It's a clear night and despite the light pollution I can see two, maybe three stars. I look out, hoping for a sign, some kind of extra twinkle, even if from an O'Hare landing beacon. "Senna," I say, my voice sounding in my head somewhere between sympathetic and defeated, "give me your hand." She shrinks against the door. "Come on, would I hit you? Give me your hand again."

I hold out my right hand, and she timidly offers me her left. I begin with the fingers, making small twists up and down each one in turn. I use my thumb to loosen the tendons on the back of her hand, then turn it over and work on the palm. I drive this way—one-handed, straining to see my beacon—all the way home.

There are nights I know I won't sleep, nights that demand I acknowledge the imbalance of my life and apply a counterweight or two. By 3 A.M. I more or less understand this: My fear for Senna's safety is just a front for my fear that when she's gone I will be lost. I should have been careful. I married a man I knew would make a wreck of my heart. I told him, Yes, he did need to follow his calling. He had to stay on the road—the music was *important*—Senna and I would make it through okay. We reasoned, we discussed. But in the end, the only compromise was mine. I'm afraid for Senna, and I envy her. She'll never be this foolish. She got her father's looks, but she'll leave a trail of awestruck boys behind her like she was a tornado.

At work, the front desk sends a call through without a name. I have to say cheerily, "Corporate Marketing, this is Sue."

"Hi, Sue Rawling? This is Dave from Azarello's"

It takes me a moment. "Oh, yes, *Trance*. You've got my work number."

He says he's calling to thank me for my purchase, wants to know how it's working out. I remind him that, actually, the drum is for Senna. He stumbles a little, but finishes his spiel: "And we've got a free class here at the store on the thirtieth, so if your . . ."

"Daughter."

"Daughter wants to come check it out, it should be really . . ."

"Fun?" Okay, I'm being mean. I throw him a bone. "How's the funk hop DJ-ing going, Dave?"

Now he's back in his element. "Elevated, every Wednesday. Ten-buck cover, but you get in free." I thank him, but no thanks. There's an awkward silence. "Cool," he says, "I'm out, Sue." I go through the morning with an amused smile on my lips. People notice, smile back.

And then I come back from lunch and check my voice mail. A message—from August. They've had a few canceled shows. He's coming home in a week.

Is it enough to say that I'm paralyzed? Exactly how do I get up each morning and go through the usual choreography, as I've done for months and months? The life I lead on my own suddenly feels irrelevant, impossible. Can I call August a significant absence when I'm the one who no longer seems present? I try to get hold of Rick, to find out where August is and when, precisely, he'll be arriving home. August doesn't carry his keys on the road; he loses little things easily.

Senna has the good sense not to go out. We cook and eat in silence, watch movies in our sweats. Most of the time she camps out in her room listening to her music and knitting. On Saturday night she meets a boy for Thai food in Uptown but comes back in less than two hours. "He was kind of low-key," she says, "and the food sucked."

"Low-key," I say, "what does that mean exactly?"

"Oh, he was fun, and really cute, but just . . . boring. No ideas, I guess. No plans."

I try not to sound derisive: "Aren't you a little young for plans?"

She pauses, seems to seriously consider this. "I'm looking for someone special."

"Special can wear you out. You'll learn to appreciate boring."

She rolls her eyes. "Sure, Mom."

When Senna goes to her room, I sit on the couch staring at the wall. I keep turning over something August said once in an

interview. *His proudest achievement?* His band. Because everyone who played sideman for him also had his own thing—some
group, some project where *he* was frontman. *August Rawling has
no hired hands.*

Yes, but when their CDs come out, if they ever do, there's always a little sticker attached: "of the August Rawling Band" or
"formerly of."

Thirty years ago, people bragged about their sister or uncle
or brother-in-law being personal secretary, gardener, caddy, you
name it, to such-and-such city alderman or some bigwig down at
Montgomery Ward. Now everyone wants to be lauded on their
own merits, adored if possible. Does getting by no longer consti-
tute a life? Thirty years ago, you were proud to be a *janitor*, to
scrub toilets in a good building, work for a good company. Now
you despise yourself for missing the chance at something better, something that might have gotten *you* featured in a magazine. Fame is never out of reach; you just didn't grab it when you
could have. You didn't quit your day job, couldn't get noticed,
no one understood you, you were ahead of your time, or behind
it, weren't pretty or charismatic or lucky or hungry or desperate
enough, didn't have money, or didn't fall in with the right people.
And then you see someone like August Rawling and it makes you
sick, because he got everything you didn't and has the bald nerve
to talk about frontmen and sidemen. Now everyone has plans, and
almost everyone is disappointed.

Sunday morning, I feel so antic I make an emergency massage
appointment. When I arrive, my usual masseuse is on vacation. I
get a new woman who uses so much oil I come out feeling like a
glazed ham.

In the clamor of my office, I hear only one voice—the voice
you take out driving with friends on Friday night, sing along to
in the shower, the voice that gets you through yet another bland,
featureless day. A voice the taste and color of tobacco, of earth, of
opium—the voice that's been with me my entire adult life.

"We're in Oklahoma. Gonna try to push through and make it
in tonight. If not, we'll do something at one of the universities.

Stop downstate somewhere. Give them a thrill. Hey, Susie . . ." the voice says, "am I coming through?"

I can't move, think, talk. I'm in love with him. That's the problem.

"I had a fight with Evie. Rick and Saul too."

Something rumbles by. They're at a truck stop. "I talked to Rick the other day. He didn't say anything about it."

"Senna got into trouble."

"Shit, what happened?"

"She's okay," I say brusquely. I suddenly don't want to involve him in it. I want to keep it between me and Senna. "We're okay."

"Susie, I know this whole thing . . ." The sound of air brakes releasing in the background drowns him out for a moment. "It's been a whirlwind. For you guys too."

It hasn't been. Not at all. The home front has been quiet. I'd take a whirlwind any day.

Either August or the truck lets out another long sigh. "I am exhausted. Played four and a half hours last night. Be nice to sleep in my bed. But these kids, Susie . . . I mean, they're really hearing it this time."

"I'm glad."

"I know I always say that. But it feels different this time." When I don't reply, he says, "We can sock it all away this time. We could retire on this one."

Doesn't work either. August, retire? And why does everyone assume I loathe my job? Up until rather recently, I've been the breadwinner.

He tries again: "Graduation is on the thirteenth, right? We throwing a party?"

"Cindy's parents. Barbecue."

"Maybe I'll bring my guitar."

"The girls are the main act, August."

"Sure. No, you're right." Over the phone, I hear someone calling his name. He calls something back. "Look, we'll make it in tonight. I'll tell Charlie to put the pedal down, make some time. Miss you guys too much. We'll push through, make it in tonight."

The room swarms back in, my coworkers chattering, the coffee pot gurgling. Tonight.

"Push through," I tell him. "Try."

I hang up, put my head in my hands, stare at my desk calendar until the dates and all the scrawled-in little notes blur together. I pick up the phone again.

"What's up, Mom?"

I ask if she has cash for the bus, tell her to meet me at Halsted and Roscoe at seven. We're going for some real Thai food. She starts to say good-bye, but I interrupt.

"Senna," I say, "one more thing. Don't forget to lock the downstairs gate."

Twenty years ago Elevated would've been a neighborhood bar filled at nine-thirty at night with serious-looking men slouching at the bar, their heads slowly descending toward tumblers of whiskey. Now it looks like a boutique furniture showroom, the kind of yuppie place August would rather piss on than patronize. This suits me just fine.

Senna and I are still snuffling and red-cheeked, bellies full of Thai curry, hopped up on strong tea. We find Trance at the bar. The dreadlocks are gone, replaced by a buzz cut. I can't decide if he looks older or younger. "Hey!" Trance says, obviously unable to put my face with a name. Perhaps he meets a lot of forty-three-year-old women as a disc jockey. But, bless him, he does remember. "Ms. Rawling . . . awesome to see you out."

"Just Sue is fine. And I told you about Senna, yes?" If I could read Senna's thoughts, and at this moment I dearly wish I could, she'd be saying, What the fuck?

The bartender looks at Senna skeptically. "It's cool, man," Trance says. "They're cool. They're with me." He leads us to a couch. "Get you ladies anything to drink?"

"A little slow tonight?" I say.

"Early. They just put a mix on till eleven, then I get up and rock the joint. So, how do you two know each other?"

"Trance," I say, "remember? My daughter?"

"Yeah," he says. He turns to Senna. "Yeah, I sold your mom a—"

"Two cherry cokes would be *great*, Trance."

He saunters across the floor and leans on the bar, scans the room with an expression on his face he must think of as smoldering, but looks more like constipated to me. I turn and give Senna a conspiratorial nudge. "Look like a good time?"

"It's a surprise."

"Let's have a good time. I want to have a good time with you tonight."

"Sure," Senna says after a moment.

Trance returns with our drinks. "We like this place," I say. "It's got atmosphere." I take a drink. Predictably, it's nearly three-quarters booze. I raise my glass to Senna. "Enjoy while it lasts, kid."

Trance clinks our glasses, tips his beer bottle back, and takes a long drink.

The rest of the night lurches ahead. I don't know where all the fresh drinks come from. I buy a few of them. Trance gets up in his little DJ pulpit and starts the room pulsing along to his records. I recognize snatches of old singles—reggae, R&B, soul—but the songs are all jumbled, sped up, slowed down, bent and twisted. Senna and I dance. She knows how to move to this music, and I try my best. For almost an hour, the floor is ours alone. We start to find a rhythm together. We loosen up, shake our asses, throw our arms up over our heads. When Trance plays Living Soul, a band I used to love in the eighties, I let out a hoot. "Jesus, Mom," Senna says, laughing and shaking her head.

Just before midnight, the room fills up with groups of men in untucked dress shirts and women in minis and furry boots. I lose Senna in the crowd and retreat to a booth in the corner. I look out into a little sea of knees, raise my drink, and drain it down to the ice. A little tremor runs through me. My stomach turns over. I know it, I feel it, I *intuit* it—Christ, did I use to believe in intuition—at this very instant August is getting back into a car—his bass player's, his soundman's—and driving away. I don't know if he realizes I've locked him out on purpose, but he is leaving confused and irritated that he'll be spending the night on someone's couch instead of in his own bed. I want him to feel this, what it's like to be the one who always has to wait.

Someone sits down next to me. A hand brushes my thigh underneath the table.

"What are you doing?" I say, "shouldn't you be—"

Trance points to the booth, where another kid is wearing a pair of headphones half on, half off, and flipping through records.

"I wanted to sit with you," he says.

"Trance, I'm a little . . . I don't really—"

"What's wrong?" he says—tender, but only interested in one thing.

"Please," I say, "Trance . . ."

For a moment the crowd sways itself apart, and I see Senna dancing by herself, beer in hand, paying no heed to the young people preening and presenting all around her. I close my eyes and try to take myself, through all the booze and bad perfume, not just out of the room but out of my body and out of this life. I try to go back to when I was her, the girl standing in the audience staring up at the boy with the acoustic guitar and the crooked nose who, at that moment, looked and sounded like nothing but promise, pure promise. I'm being silly, I tell myself. Hysterical. The second I see him, none of this will matter. I feel my legs readying themselves to lift me from this haze, to rush home, hoping I haven't missed him.

The hand brushes my thigh again. "I'm glad you came tonight," Trance says. I turn and look at him.

"Why don't you go talk to her?" I say thickly. "Go dance."

"I want to talk to you."

"Isn't she . . . Isn't she pretty enough? Go on. She likes boys like you."

"I like you."

He touches me between my legs. I shudder. I breathe more heavily. Is this meant to encourage him? I really don't know. No good will come of this moment, but it won't be just another footnote in the August Rawling story. I lean over, kiss Trance on the cheek. His stubble is rougher than August's.

"She's plain," Trance murmurs. "You're special."

It takes me a moment too long to respond. "Wrong," I say, weak as water. "Wrong." I put my hand on top of his searching hand and hold it there. I find my daughter in the crowd. She's still dancing, lost in her own world. "Enjoy it while it lasts," I murmur. The music keeps thumping away. I start his hand moving again, close my eyes, and wait until he thinks it's over.

Tonight no longer matters. Endings are easy, it's the rest—tomorrow, the months to follow—that terrifies me. Home is cool and quiet, Senna too drunk to undress herself. I hold her hair back as she vomits into the toilet. When I get her into bed, she's pale but clear-eyed again.

"Senna," I say, "stay with me another minute. I have something for you." I go into my bedroom, shove some clothes aside, and pull the drum out of the closet. I wrap my arms around the thing, waver on my feet in the darkness.

"A gift from mother to daughter," I say as I set it down beside her bed. "Something she can take wherever she goes."

Senna smiles faintly. "I found it the other day. I was trying your dresses on."

"I'll get you a traveling bag. You can play it on the top of the Himalayas."

"I love it, Mom . . ."

My mouth opens in protest before she even says it.

"I'll have to leave it here. It's too big."

She's right, I realize. I bought this thing hoping to anchor her, not set her free.

"I'm passing out, Mom." Her eyes flutter closed.

"I'm going to go a little crazy when you leave. You know that, don't you?"

She's with me again. For some reason, I expect her to be crying. She's not.

"You and Dad don't have to stay together for my sake."

"Senna—" I say, scolding. And then something in me folds up and packs itself away, and I tell her, "He's not going anywhere just yet."

I can't keep him out of my life. Nothing changes. We just have to remind ourselves, now and then, how we live with our lives. Maybe I've learned how to be the supporting cast so that Senna won't have to. A nice thought anyway.

"Why don't you learn to play the drum, Mom?" She really is drunk. I have to smile.

"I'm too old," I say softly and pull the covers over her. "It's too embarrassing."

Me, I wait backstage until the storm of applause finally withdraws, until the lights go up and they've all gone home. That's me — the one who's always there at the end of the night. And tonight I'm tucking my daughter into bed, and in the morning I'm hauling myself up and I'm going to work. Someone gets to do that too.

Dead
Weight

They came from Overland Park, Kansas. Burgs like that swarm with kids with nothing to do but sit around practicing their instruments, playing along to shitty metal records after school and throwing shapes in the mirror till Mom calls them down for Jennie-O turkey loaf, Stove Top stuffing, and apple pie out of the box. VD3 hadn't played more than a handful of shows in Chicago before they had A&R guys sniffing their butts. Justin and Jayson—that's who they wanted. The twins looked like they'd been concocted in some secret lab buried deep in the vanilla heart of America. Threatless rebellion, good teeth, and the promise of heavy petting at the end of the night—the twins were the zeitgeist all right. They were going to move some units.

Marty and Thomas, on the other hand . . . Well, they were nice guys. Marty, at twenty-two, already had a bald spot. He should've been training to sell insurance or maybe vinyl siding door-to-door, not playing bass in a band. Thomas, the drummer, was a shaggy, slope-shouldered oaf. He reminded you of one those big dogs that roll side-to-side when they walk and like to flop down anywhere and fall asleep in the sun, one of those dogs you'd have to put down early, health problems inherent in the breed. You'd feed him cheese, his favorite, and he'd lick your hand while the vet slid the needle in, and afterward you'd all smile bravely and agree you'd done the right thing.

I first met the dead weight in the studio, before I'd even laid eyes on the twins. VD3 had hooked up with the same management company who handled Disturbed, that god-awful "nü-metal" band from the south side that went on to sell six million records. The management was priming VD3 for a deal and wanted them to cut some demos at Rax Trax. After two days, they were telling both Marty and Thomas they needed someone "steadier" to lay down the parts. The job came to me from a buddy who did a lot of studio work but couldn't make the date. Up till then, I'd stayed as far from the industry as I could. I was a little naive myself. I didn't know what I was walking into. These four kids had spent the last seven years holed up in a garage on some leafy side street pounding out these songs, practicing to play basement parties and their high school talent show. I had to go in and lay down Thomas's parts while he stood on the other side of the glass, watching intently, thinking he was going to pick up some tips from a real pro. "Thanks, man," he said when I was done. "I really learned a lot."

Thank God I wasn't there when they told them, when the contract was drawn up without their names on it. (From what I heard, Justin and Jayson weren't there either; they'd handed the hard stuff over to the pros as well.) Six months after they'd come to the big city to try and make it with their band, Marty and Thomas were being sent home to Kansas, enough payoff money in their pockets for a new car or a down payment on a townhouse, enough to keep them from kicking up a fuss about who wrote which songs.

When VD3 signed to Universal, I was sent out to LA to track the album. On "Subliminal Vengeance," "Krazy Girrrl," "Hooded Justice," "Tragedies of the Silent," and "OMG, So N2U," I played almost exactly what Thomas (a pretty good drummer, it turned out) did on their home recordings, and my other parts weren't spectacularly different from the originals either. I played on half the album, and they flew in Josh Freese to do the rest. Afterward, the whole thing was so quantized, compressed, resampled, and chopped up on Pro Tools it hardly seemed to matter who'd actually hit the drums in the first place.

How can I describe this music? It managed to meld everything popular on the radio—metal riffs, skittery electronic beats, melodramatic breakdown sections, white-boy rapping, self-help lyrics, and endless, yelping iterations of the word *girl*—into one market-conquering protogenre. Thanks to some sophisticated recording software, it sounded glossy and crunchy, slick and jagged, sensitive and angry all at once. The sound track to your next teenage riot, and Grandma could still buy it for you for Christmas.

Over two weeks in LA, I spoke to Justin and Jayson a handful of times, only the occasional "What's up, bro?" and "Sounding good, Tim. Totally ripping on those tracks." They were like Siegfried and Roy's white tigers—beasts of such rarefied breeding you were amazed to see them suffer our harsh climate. As with all identical twins, you secretly tried to spot the minor differences, who got the shorter draw in the genetic lottery. All I could pick out was that Jayson walked with a slight limp (old snowboarding injury), and Justin, the obsessive one, liked to chew on the plastic fob on his keychain.

The twins had just turned twenty-two, but there was already a coldness to them, a lofty distance. They needed that coldness, I guess. Probably someone had explained it to them: how it was painful but inevitable that the original lineup should part ways. This wasn't the garage anymore. This wasn't the talent show.

I came back to Chicago, back to cocktail jobs, straight-ahead gigs at the Mill and the Showcase, and free and out sessions—postbop, skronk, postskronk—in loft spaces and coffeehouses. I socked away my $15,000 and considered my little excursion into mall rock over. Then I got a call from the management company. "Tim," they said, "we want you to do the tour. The concept is: This needs to look like a real band. Four comrades who'll fight to the end and die for each other. Justin and Jayson love your sound and your look, and we need someone who isn't known on the national scene. Who are you working with right now?" I told them I was playing with some of the biggest names in the Chicago jazz community. "Perfect," they said. "No one will ever have heard of you."

They'd lined up another Chicago cat, Paul Patton, to play bass. (I'd heard of Paul—a session guy who kept a low profile, a monster on his instrument—and was even a little flattered to be paired with him.) They had promoters prebooking shows, street teams flyering the clubs, media people blitzing radio and magazines, new media people hanging out in forums and courting the bloggers.

I remember walking out of my apartment and seeing posters plastered all up and down Milwaukee Avenue: "VD3—*Pillars of Society*" scrawled in a jagged script and the band shot from below to make everyone tough and looming, the black eye shadow, leather bracelets, and dyed, spiked, tipped, and teased hair adding up to a look that seemed equal parts vampire and drug addict but finally, thanks to the weird makeup, suggested something more like "psycho mime." Justin and Jayson stood glowering and airbrush-beautiful in front. In the back, submerged in shadow, was Paul. And next to him, sulking in the same getup, me.

I should explain: My trip has never been about money, though I'm proud to scrape out a living playing music. How many of us can ever hope for an honest shot at transcendence? There had been moments on the bandstand, in the cauldron of group improvisation, when I'd start to have this feeling like I was floating out of myself, when my feet and hands and fingers and mind were working with such simultaneity that there was almost no *me* left. And on a very few occasions, four or five at most, I'd literally been able to look down upon myself and see all my mistakes and flaws, but also my skill and perfection. In that hard-won, incredibly rare set of moments, I'd known myself with a thoroughness, a *detail*, that hardly anyone ever even senses. The tour: I was going to use VD3 for the cash, to set myself up for the next year and maybe longer, to keep playing the angry, pure, fire-breathing jazz I loved and couldn't live without.

We did a warm-up show at Metro. Capacity crowd. All ages, of course. Probably half the kids got in free, having worked all weekend flyering the album. We played with spine-thrumming volume. I don't know how those kids could take it. The bass drum echoing off the back wall was like getting shelled in a bunker. Onstage, we had in-ear monitors, the whole thundering mix piped through a tiny pair of isolating headphones. It was strange. I hit the drums as hard as I could—I heard them, but they seemed to produce no sound. The whole instrument disappeared in front of me.

We flew out east and played a string of ten- to fifteen-thousand-seat houses, "sold out" on every marquee. I had to give it to Justin and Jayson. There was no learning curve for them. From the first downbeat, they thrashed around the stage like eels going upstream. Every night on the last song of the set, they'd turn to the drum riser, lean back in the heroic rock straddle, and play their matching SG guitars like it truly, truly mattered, smiling and nodding at me and Paul like we'd all been doing this together for years, like we were really locked in. The first few shows I played with incredible concentration. If there was any nuance in those songs, I was going to wring it out of them. Then I realized the sound guys were gating my drums. No matter how deftly I played, only the loud, basic stuff would come through. It would sound exactly the same every night. So I gave up on all the subtle drags, ghost notes, and over-the-bar fills. I just hit my parts, tried not to fuck up, and let the back of the house worry about the rest.

Not that it mattered much if I fucked up. There was a backing track playing the whole time, the album versions of the songs mixed in with the live sound, just loud enough so the audience wouldn't notice if you dropped a few bars or broke a stick. "Sound reinforcement," they call it. In other words—playing along with the record.

It was written in our contracts that we wouldn't get so drunk or high before or during the show that we'd let all the kids down. I couldn't drink beer behind the drums, just Aquafina brand bottled water. "I thought this was a rock tour," I said to Paul. He did two or three of these seventy-, eighty-night engagements a year. "Where are the coked-up groupies and the hot tubs full of champagne?"

"That's a story from another era. Anyway," he said, shrugging, "we're not the big show. You and me, we're just window dressing."

By the time we hit the hotel bar, Paul was usually in his room playing Xbox or talking on the phone with his wife. Even the twins indulged only as a sort of courtesy, drinking a few beers and exiting the party around one in the morning. They were constantly assaulted by girls, a good number of whom held dubious claims to being twenty-one. But Justin and Jayson were chaste. They both had girlfriends in Chicago who were coming out to join the second half of the tour.

Back then I could still more or less pass for twenty-five, but for the girls at those parties I was a target of secondary importance. Still, there were always a few women—beautiful women, glamorous and bored with their provincial lives—who seemed content to settle for the drummer. (You know what they say about drummers: half the ego, twice the stamina.) They flirted brazenly, made it clear they were here because, tonight, this was the best thing going in Scranton or Raleigh or Virginia Beach, the only party where you might brush up against reckless youth and fame, feel a little of its essence tingling your skin. "So, tell me, honestly," these women said, leaning forward confidentially, expertly, on stiletto heels, "can you really tell the two of them apart?"

"Oh, totally," I said. "After all these years, absolutely." After a couple weeks, and several drinks, I got good at inventing a VD3 history: the first scrappy practices, the basements, the house parties, and then the triumphant battle of the local bands, followed swiftly by the big-city wake-up call, slugging it out in rat-hole clubs, working hard, stitching together a following one fan at a time. . . .

"This must be so huge for you." A strategic touch on my arm transferred a charge so erotic and desperate I shivered all over. "You must be so nervous up there."

"No, why?"

"After so much work and effort, it must be nerve-wracking."

"Oh, well, you just kind of roll with it."

At a certain point, we moved the conversation to my hotel room, both of us making it clear we regarded the whole thing from the proper ironic distance. And generally it was as it should be: two adults screwing toward oblivion, then adding each other on MySpace afterward.

We flew out west and picked up a new tour bus. The first thing Paul did was block out the world by taping pictures of his wife, his newborn kid, and their apartment in Roscoe Village to his window. You're crazy, I thought. From my seat, my little area, I liked to take in the scenery, see the amber waves of grain, the filling stations, outlet malls, the purple mountain majesties ticking by. Pretty soon it got depressing. So much of this country feels all but abandoned.

In Seattle, a couple hours before the show, I was in the green room, working rudiments on the practice pad, my strokes sloppy, sticks clacking all over the place. Justin wandered in. I think it was Justin anyway. He was chewing on his keychain fob. White tiger gnawing on a hunk of meat. Several empty beers and a full one sat next to me, and I made an "uh oh" face. He just shrugged.

"Great show last night, man," I said. Around them, I was always aware that I was talking to my boss. Keep the leader happy—first rule of playing music. "Dug your solo on 'Mission Akomplished.' Man, it was so fucking . . . precise."

"Yeah, that show was off the chain. What a rad crowd."

I thought to leave it there, leave it like my other passing encounters with the twins. But he looked so morose. "What's up? Everything okay?"

"Just feeling run-down."

"The road can catch up quicker than you think." I did my best to sound like the experienced veteran proffering hard-won advice. "Make sure to take your vitamins. The food sucks." Actually, the catering beat what I ate at home by a long shot.

"For real. If I even see another crab puff . . ."

"Oh, man, those crab puffs? They're good at first. But they give you wicked gas."

We both laughed. I figured I'd scored a point or two.

"It's just . . ." He stared at his shoes — Vans, they were sponsoring the tour. "I'm just a little lonely is all. There's no one to talk to."

"Lonely? You've got Jayson here. And your girlfriends are coming out in a couple days, right?"

"Yeah, they're gonna meet us at the Shoreline show. But it's . . . tough. It's really tough." He was at a loss. "You know?"

"It can grind you down. But stay strong. Remember who you're doing it for. You're doing it for the kids. For the fans."

"Right," he said, mechanically scuffing the top of one shoe with the other, so they didn't look brand-new. "Because just a few years ago, *we* were those kids out there watching our heroes onstage. And now we gotta give it back. We gotta show them anything's possible."

"*Exactly.* That's why you have to stay strong. Anything's possible." I let out a sudden giggle. "And stay away from those crab puffs."

"What?" he said, bewildered, his thoughts still elsewhere. "Oh, right."

That night I rode the sound reinforcement hard, dropped my sticks twice doing some idiot twirling during "Antiseptic Apocalypse." The twins both shot me a look at the same time, and I dug in and finished the set without missing a single hit. That night I discovered another rule of the road: Stop pretending it's art; go on muscle memory.

In LA, we played the Roxy and then a secret show up in the hills. Backstage, there were Hollywood types. In particular, a young actress I couldn't take my eyes off. You'd know her by name. She's in those kinds of movies that, our society being efficient at mass punishment, literally everyone has seen. The ones where the guy never recognizes the girl until she takes off her brunette wig and she's not really the local meteorologist but a big star. Somehow I went up and talked to her. Or she came over and talked to me. Things, especially time, got a little jumbled. We found a room. She gave me a pill.

"What is it?" I asked.

"It doesn't really have a name yet. *Everyone's* doing them though."

I don't know how to describe what it did to me. It was like I had a head and a body. Understand me? A head. And a body. The only thing connecting me was a long filament down which I'd send signals. It was like those rare, beautiful times on the bandstand when I could look down and see myself—but this came on instantly. Those years of solitude and frustration and endless repetition weren't required after all. I felt a roar of anger welling up inside me. But after a few minutes I didn't care. The filament trailed off so distantly I couldn't feel the end anymore. At this point, the young actress pulled off my jeans and climbed on top of me. We began to fuck, and it was like one glacier colliding with another glacier, an age or two passing while all that slow, awful pressure ground itself down, like the singing of a knife being drawn along a whetstone of unimaginable length.

"What does your name mean?" she said.

"What, Tim? Timothy? Timotheos? It means"—I somehow knew to let a significant pause hang in the air—"It means, 'God's honor.'"

"No, the band name."

"Oh . . . It's just something you come up with when you're fifteen, you know? Something that sounds cool."

"I thought it was, like, the name of a missile. Something subversive. Antiwar."

"For real."

The only thought I could form: Not one in a million—maybe one in ten million—men would ever find themselves in the position I was in, there underneath that young actress. I'd done it. I'd made the peak. And now I was looking out across all humanity, from such a height that the vast populations spread out around me were faceless, featureless, their heads bobbing and waving in the great winds of time like tassels of corn, ready for the reaping hand. And I thought: What does it matter who remembers us when we die? Who cares what songs we try to play? I still had my shoes on, but I thought, What has happened to my feet?

On the bus, Jayson came hitching his snowboarding-maimed leg down the aisle. I had a wet towel over my face, trying to shut out the world. I'd used up a month's worth of serotonin in one night. Over the next week, we were heading back to the heartland, the desolation of Oklahoma City, Topeka, Des Moines. . . . Chicago was in sight, but it seemed impossible I'd ever get back.

"Have fun last night?" Jayson said, sitting down next to me. This new familiarity pretty well stunned me. Then again, we'd been playing in a band together for the last two and a half months. "Everyone says she loves drummers. She collects them I guess." He leaned over, took an ice pack from the minifridge, wrapped it in a towel.

"So what's wrong with you?" I said. Maybe I didn't really know their tastes after all. Maybe he and Justin were having the real parties back in their room.

"Shit, I'm cool. Just this fucking headache." Now I really was shocked. The twins hardly ever swore. "We're playing KC on Friday night."

"Oh, right, hometown show. Getting psyched?"

"Yeah," he said, wincing at the cold of the ice pack, "it'll rock." Then he looked at me, directly at me, and I felt myself falling into those gray Siberian eyes. "Hey, Tim, how'd you get started in music? Or, I mean, why?"

"Why did I *start* playing music?" Jesus, it seemed I'd been doing it all my life. "I guess it was just something I was good at. Probably the only thing. I liked performing, wanted to be noticed. Maybe it's coming from a small town. And music seemed really pure. Like all you had to do was learn the song, get it perfect, get it all under your hands, and then you were absolutely free."

Jayson nodded, taking this in. "I think I wanted to get through to people," he said. "You know? Really reach them."

"Oh, sure. That too. Spooky," I said. "That's pretty much what Justin told me, as well." At the sound of his name, his brother came back and joined us. I lost track of who was who. "Do you both get headaches at the same time?" I knew those kinds of questions annoyed them but couldn't help myself. "How does that work anyway?"

"We're not telepathic," one of them said, and they both rolled their eyes.

"But that's how it is with you guys," I insisted. "I mean, *spooky*, right? Okay, tell me, what am I thinking right now?"

"We can't read *your* mind."

"Ah ha, so you admit it! You can read each other's thoughts. Okay, both of you think of a number."

"3!" Jayson said. "69!" Justin answered, gnawing happily on his keychain fob.

"What's your brother's favorite color?"

"Pink!" they both called out at the same time. I looked over at Paul, who was leaning over the back of the seat in front of him, smiling and shaking his head at all this nonsense. One of the girlfriends came back, a sweet, very pretty girl studying business at Northwestern who seemed to be, of all things, a true fan of the music. She put her arm around Jayson.

"How do you tell them apart?" I said to her. "Try not to get mixed up!"

"Well," she said, "Jayson is the more sensitive, intellectual type. Justin is brooding and intense." We all laughed. She was quoting a profile that had just run in *Seventeen*. I'd been wanting to mock it for days and felt a little deflated that someone had beaten me to it.

"But seriously, guys," Justin said, addressing Paul and me, "we just wanted to thank you for making this such a great tour. Our first tour. We couldn't have asked for a steadier rhythm section. You guys have been rock solid. A real pleasure to work with."

Paul gave them a manful nod of recognition. He'd heard this sort of speech before, no doubt. But I couldn't help feeling moved. If the bus burst into flames right then, at least I'd made ten- to fifteen-thousand ticket-holders happy every night for the last three months.

You'd have thought nothing ever happened in Kansas until VD3 came sailing back home. There were spots for the local news. Some old guy with a mustache, a shellacked hairdo, and a buffalo-shaped belt buckle put a microphone in front of me and asked, "Where do you get your inspiration?" I tried to be sincere about it: "My bandmates are great—fine musicians. And the songs, well, they're expertly written."

When I got to the green room, there was a middle-aged couple talking with Justin and Jayson, a large, bearded man in a corduroy sport coat and a broad-shouldered woman wrapped in a peacock shawl: Mom and Dad with their vampire-mime twins, in a quiet moment before the big show. Justin and Jayson called me over. I shook hands, and Dad said, "Now, you're making sure my boys stay out of trouble, aren't you?" And I was about to say, "I wouldn't worry about them, they're pros," when another large, sweaty palm was being thrust in front of me and someone was saying,

"Tim, what's up, man? Hey, I saw some video of you guys playing in Denver. Awesome. You're really killing it up there!"

I was already reaching for the Sharpie in my pocket when I realized it was Thomas, the shaggy dog I'd been called in to put down eight months ago. "For fuck's sake, it's been a while, bro!" I even hugged him, so carried away was I by a quicksilver spirit of generosity and reconciliation. "How you been keeping, man?"

He nodded his head abidingly. "Not bad, not bad." He wasn't as tall or as oafish as I remembered. He'd lost some weight. There were dark circles under his eyes.

"Is Marty here too?"

"He couldn't make it tonight."

Brave kid, coming here by himself, coming to wish his former bandmates good luck. Or maybe he just couldn't keep himself away, he had to get one glimpse. I could see him, trying his hardest not to look around the room, trying not to see the spread of gourmet food, the champagne, the nineteen-thousand-dollar Les Paul Custom thrown casually on the couch. From the corridor outside, we could already hear the laughter of the twenty or so girls who'd been given backstage passes.

"You gonna catch the show?" I asked him.

"Oh, yeah. Justin and Jayson hooked me up. Front row center." He smiled; his eyes were bright, fixed on me. Christ, the stoicism of the Plains! I thought of frontier settlers slugging it out through droughts, famines, and killing winters, all for some stony parcel of land. They were used to sacrificing themselves out here. They were used to dying quiet.

The parents had gone off somewhere. Justin and Jayson had moved across the room and were talking with the tour manager. They kept looking over at us nervously. Thomas kept glancing at them. A gulf had opened up, and I could feel the three of them silently straining to reach each other. But there seemed no way now to cross over. Thomas had been fobbed off on me for a little shoptalk, drummer to drummer.

"Cool, man, cool," I said. "So, you been playing? Working on any new projects?"

"Me and Marty have been jamming on some new stuff. It's hard to describe. There are all kinds of elements. Some blues elements, some funk, some rock."

"Sick. Sounds eclectic."

"Yeah, we're drawing on a lot of different influences. I'm doing some singing."

"Don Henley–style."

"Exactly. But way different." He gave me a pained, apologetic smile. "We were gonna start playing out, but Marty, he's not doing so good. He moved back in with his mom. It's sort of like, since everything happened . . ."

At that point, the tour manager let the girls outside in the corridor into the room, and suddenly we were drowned out by excited laughter. Now Thomas couldn't keep his eyes from roaming. I watched him taking stock of it all, his face twitching as he looked at the girls. This would be the closest he'd get. Seeing it now, feeling that vicarious rush before the show, it would wither up the rest of his life. Whenever people saw his dusty drum kit stacked up in the basement or garage and asked, Do you still play? he'd have to say, Not in years. He'd have to laugh at himself, his adolescent fantasies, striking poses in the mirror.

"I'd better eat something and start warming up. The catering is pretty awful, way too rich," I added, as if my professional gripes were any consolation to him.

"Right on, man," Thomas said. "Warming up is totally key, right?"

"Totally."

To my dismay, he stayed backstage, talking to the roadies, trying to engage a few nervous-looking girls in conversation as their eyes darted around him, looking for an exit. He caught me again just as I was going onstage.

"Hey, Tim, maybe if I'm ever back in Chicago, I can take a lesson from you."

"You got it." I slapped him on the shoulder. "Anytime, brother."

I counted off the first song. Paul's bass kicked in like a concussion round lobbed over the horizon. Justin and Jayson seemed skittish, but they played with a ferociousness I hadn't seen before. The tempos started to creep up. We were all a few beats ahead of the backing track, and it sounded like a mess. Paul looked over at me, and we tried to lock in. For "Mission Akomplished" and "Hooded Justice," he and I tried to split the difference between what the twins were playing and the recorded track, tried to drag them back into time. I had the click track bing-bonging in my ear the whole time and was doing my best to ignore it. Then one of the guys in the crew ran out between songs and told me they were cutting the sound reinforcement altogether.

From the corner of my eye, I could see Thomas standing in the wings, watching.

"Jesus, all right," I said. "Shit. Let's play some music then." And then I counted off "Krazy Girrrl," and we slammed into the opening chords.

Off the chain. That's what the twins always said. But this really was off the chain, snarling and lunging like some wild beast untethered. After a couple songs, I found myself singing along. They were pop songs, after all. Big and dumb. They even had a sting to them, like sugar hitting a nerve under your gums. We were playing those songs the way they must have sounded when VD3 first wrote them, when they were just four surly, pent-up kids down in the basement, playing for the hell of it, any dreams of stardom so remote and idealized they were just the gauzy prelude to turkey loaf and the first fading of youth.

It started to happen: all thought and conscious effort dropped away. True independence. My two feet operating separately from my two hands, each limb its own perfect machine. I didn't think verse, chorus, fill, bridge, stop-time, fill. I just played. After three more songs, I could feel myself rising. It was real this time, not some chemical. I glanced over at Thomas again. I closed my eyes and fought as hard as I could. It was almost impossible to come back down.

We hit the last chords of "Vengeance." The crowd roared up like a typhoon. Justin was already starting the song with his stuttering rhythm part. I shouted over to the wings, held up my sticks, waved to Thomas to come over to the drums. *Come on, get out here.* He stood there looking confused, but then a thought dawned on him—this must be part of the act, a surprise reunion for the hometown crowd.

I beckoned to him again, but he just stood there, smiling at me helplessly, too bashful or too goddamn sensible to go out there and hit some drums. The management had been right. You couldn't have gotten him and Marty up in front of twenty thousand people in the first place.

I missed my entrance. The twins turned to the drum riser, a questioning look mirrored on their faces. I put my in-ear monitors back in and picked up the beat in the middle of the verse.

No one seemed to notice the fuck-up. They'd faded the sound reinforcement back in. I played the rest of the song lined up with it perfectly, note for note. We all did. We played perfectly. The fans were not disappointed.

Mr. Fern,
Freestyle

He heard them as he was coming around the corner. They were gathered at the church steps, as they often were before rehearsal. He stopped just out of sight and listened. They were trading back and forth, improvising:

> Mr. Fern, he wild
> Rockin' pleats and loafers
> In the Cosby style

> Sippin' on Mylanta, chewin' on Tums
> Mr. Fern, sorry I'm late . . .
> Just don't call my moms!

Mr. Fern, where my iPod
Took that shit three months back
Anything come out that desk . . .
You gotta pray to God

Mr. Fern . . . got a wife with one leg
Every night before bed
He gotta bust out the Pledge!

At that last one, they all broke up laughing. *Oh, snap, snap! Bella, that's ill! That's too ill!* Mr. Fern came around the corner then, and—*Oh, shit, busted*—the group scattered and flew inside. The three guilty ones stood there, caught, but unsure how much he'd heard. Marshall and Ty looked at the ground, but Bella—ugly, chalky Bella—stared him in the face, defying him to say anything.

"All right, all right," Mr. Fern said, "that's enough fooling around. Get in there and get warming up." He shooed them in front of him. "Five minutes. Five minutes and you'd better be in those robes and ready to sing."

Rehearsal went badly. It was a rare warm October evening, and the bells of the ice cream vendors and the long, heavy bass notes rumbling from cars on nearby corners came floating through the open windows. Little pockets of chatter kept opening up among the choir. He sought out the perpetrators, gave them hard, warning looks. And then he couldn't help his gaze drifting to Ty and Bella in the altos and Marshall in the baritones. Of the three, only Marshall could sing, though he persisted in a strange, pseudo-operatic vibrato. Either he was making mockery, or that really was what he thought good singing sounded like. As for the other two, Mr. Fern had given Ty a tambourine to play and Bella an egg-shaped shaker, hoping that would make them feel they were contributing and keep them from singing so loudly. It had worked with Ty, but Bella continued to belt it out in a flagrantly bored monotone.

Mr. Fern delivered a lecture on head voice. He briefly demonstrated, singing an $E4$ from his chest and then his head, and then, in pure, unwavering voice, sliding up an octave to $E5$. Several of the older boys snickered; Mr. Fern cut the demonstration short. He rarely sang in front of the group these days—they seemed to not even *want* to learn. Half-consciously, he reached down and smoothed the front of his trousers. He was, indeed, wearing pleats that day. Just the night before Regina had sat down with her sewing machine and let out the waist.

Outside the light was failing, but he kept the choir twenty minutes late to work on "Beulah Land." That Sunday they would have to perform twice, and he wouldn't let them go unprepared. Just before he excused them, the far door of the hall opened, and Reverend Williams looked in, waved, smiled, put his hands together, and bowed to the choir in praise. This was usually the Reverend's sign for Mr. Fern to stop by his office after rehearsal. But that evening, Mr. Fern took his time gathering up his scores and cleaning up behind the kids—after fifteen years with the church, his own unofficial way of saying he just wanted to go home. By the time he was finished, the Reverend had locked up and was gone.

"Let their teachers worry about their minds," he told Regina that night. "And the Reverend can look after their souls. I just want them to sing. They seem to think it's some kind of punishment."

Regina stood before the closet in her nightgown, choosing clothes for work the next day: a slender black pantsuit, a wide-collared blouse, vermilion heels that set the outfit off perfectly. She dressed as strikingly now as she did before the accident, back when she was still intent on performing. For the last ten years, she'd worked in a gleaming, marble-floored showroom in the Loop, selling baby grands to rich suburbanites.

"Well, for the Lord's sake, and your own," Regina said, "don't go turning it into a punishment."

"It's the three of them who are the most trouble," he went on. "They have a little group. Rap, of course." The disdain, the contempt—he was tired even of his own voice sometimes. What did his father used to say about rap? *It's not music, it's just shouting.* "'Apostles' they call themselves. Not 'The Apostles.' Just 'Apostles.' I've been corrected before."

"The car's been making that sound again. Not sure I can take another week walking and bussing all the way downtown. Sore enough as it is."

He told her he'd take the car in for service as soon as he could, next weekend maybe. "They're undermining my authority," he went on, "and ultimately they're hurting the choir. I swear, these days, standing up there in front of them, it's like being on trial."

She sat on the edge of the bed, pulled the hem of her night-gown to midthigh, and undid two snaps. With a soft pop of the suction releasing, she took off her leg, and then she rolled off the two long socks that covered her stump. She leaned over, pulled out the dresser drawer, and laid the leg in the nest of old T-shirts she'd made for it.

"It hurt today?"

"Today was a good day. Well, just a little," she amended as she worked herself under the covers. She turned and whispered in his ear, "Everything's just a little sore today."

He fit his body around hers, pressed his right thigh against her stump, rubbed against it the way she liked. The rough, scabby skin still disgusted him, but he kept going and finally found himself turned on, by a sense of his own unflagging faithfulness and generosity as much as anything. He despised himself for this egotism, and yet there it was. They made love, Regina pushed up in the corner with her hands against the wall to support her, him coming in a little sideways, the way they'd learned to do. When she came, her stump twitched and traced circles in the air, as if that leg were trying to kick out. They both fell back into bed, exhausted. As he was floating away into sleep, what Bella had said that afternoon came back. *Every night before bed, he gotta bust out the Pledge.* The idea of him polishing a wooden leg night after night . . . He couldn't keep a laugh escaping his lips. Regina stirred.

"Hmmm?"

"Nothing," he said, and then, "Sorry."

"Sorry about what?" she said sleepily.

He let her drift off without an answer.

Reverend Williams was preaching about retribution. The seductiveness of retribution. He made reference to Jacob and Esau, a part of the Bible Mr. Fern found maddening: Jacob's deceptions rewarded, God's and Isaac's judgments seemingly arbitrary, the truces between brothers hard-won and uneasy. Regina hadn't come to service that morning. She only attended once a month or so, said she found the Reverend's preaching too high-toned. Today she would've felt compelled to stay for the funeral — a boy she'd hardly known but would've wept over anyway. Mr. Fern sat to one side of the pulpit, letting the words of the eulogy slide in and out of his attention. He faced the mourners, the mothers and grandmothers wearing little round hats, big floppy hats, hats with feathers, wiping at their eyes, sniffling like they were suffering colds. It wasn't yet time for the big displays.

Out of the corner of his eye, he saw the far door open and a file of six teenage boys come down the outside aisle and work themselves into the first available row. Only the briefest pause in the Reverend's eulogy, only the slightest hitch, but Mr. Fern could feel it spread across the room, tears suddenly dried, breaths held, hands clasped more tightly. The young men wore dress shirts tucked clumsily into baggy jeans; four of them wore red ties — even here they showed their colors. Mr. Fern watched their faces. He saw the anger, and the fear. Dumb, dead James lay up there in his box, too shot up for his mother to see his face one last time. It had only been six months since the neighborhood gathered to bury another of its young men. Anger and fear, but was there regret? Was there shame on those young faces? He had to look away. He couldn't stand to see them.

When had this coldness entered him, this absence? It often frightened, sometimes thrilled him — he tested its boundaries, all the things it could nullify, could make numb and ghostly. He'd come to think of Regina's accident as the end of his belief. But maybe there'd always been something in him he held apart. Maybe when he was younger he'd simply confused religious feeling with those things that came so naturally from music: mystery, weightlessness, the unbidden response, the melody that burst forth, that asked no obedience, that couldn't help but display all its brilliance.

The Reverend turned to him. He started forward, his chair legs squeaking on the shining wood floor. He'd almost forgotten himself, his duties. Rising, he motioned for the choir to rise. As if on his cue, the women let loose. The choir's singing cannoned off the walls of the church—*I'm kind of homesick for a country / to which I've never been before*—and the wailing of the women, the sound he hated, leapt up to meet it.

He knocked on the Reverend's door.

"Come on in, Asa."

"Knew it would be me?"

The Reverend gestured to the chair across from his desk. "I saw the look on your face when those boys walked in. Figured you'd be in to talk." He sighed, scratched his bald head.

"Why do you let them in? They're a danger just sitting there among those good people."

"I hope we give them something to think about, seeing that coffin up there."

"I could see them thinking—thinking about how they're going to even up the score."

A barely eaten container of cottage cheese sat on the corner of the desk. Over the last six months, the Reverend had lost plenty of weight—said he was on a diet, good for him—but the large man and his large presence were gone, shriveled up.

"If we want to bring them into the light, Asa, we can't hide it from them."

From the larger man, these words would've sounded as truths. From the skinnier man, they were like crutches.

"James had a strong voice," Mr. Fern said. "Might have made a soloist out of him. Wish his folks could've heard him."

Keeping these children locked up in church an hour and a half twice a week—he just didn't have enough to offer them. He tried to teach a little music theory, maybe set one or two on the path to teaching music in school someday—if the schools hadn't cut music completely by then. He spent a little extra time on the most talented, tried to nurture a true voice when he heard one. There'd been successes: He'd taken the choir to statewide competitions and won first prize three years running. He'd had a protégé sing at Carnegie Hall. But that had all been years ago, and those miracles seemed now to have been worked by a different man.

"Marshall, Ty, and Bella—they've been making trouble again," Mr. Fern said, as if still on the subject of the wayward. He worried most about Marshall. Ty was safe for a little while—until his voice broke, he wouldn't be able to hang with the older boys in the neighborhood. Still, it wouldn't be much longer until he lost them both, until Marshall's mother and Ty's grandmother couldn't control them and the two boys started doing what they liked on Wednesday and Sunday. Most of the girls in the choir lasted through their teens; his boys were gone by thirteen or fourteen. Well, he'd be stuck with Bella anyway.

"Ah, yes," the Reverend said and permitted himself a smile, "our artists-in-residence. The Apostles."

"Just 'Apostles.' I've been corrected."

"They came in to see me the other day. I wanted to speak with you about it. They wanted some funds. To record an album. A demo, they called it."

Mr. Fern shook his head. "Jesus . . ."

"Now come on, Asa. I listened to what they had to say. They can be very persuasive."

"You're giving them money?"

"A hundred dollars."

"Well, that won't get them anywhere."

The Reverend put up his hands, begged off. For a moment, he looked boyish, mischievous. "I'm afraid I don't know much about these kinds of things . . ."

"Oh, no — no way — " Mr. Fern shoved out his own hands, trying to push back this sudden intrusion. "You're not getting me hooked into this."

"I recall you have some recording equipment, from back in your performing days."

It was true. For over ten years, he'd sung in Living Soul, an eight-piece R&B band that worked all over the city. He'd recorded two of the band's albums in his basement, in a little studio he'd built for the purpose. The group had won some critical acclaim, and Asa Fern, specifically, had been cited for his presence, his cool command of the stage, the way he frostily surveyed the first verses of a song, laying out a case for sorrow, hardship, even despair, deliberately, inarguably, right up to the point where the horn section began to swell, the bass dropped to its E string, the drummer hit a rim shot, and suddenly that voice leapt out of him, that high pure voice he'd been holding back so long, and all at once the audience gave itself over.

It seemed like it would last and last. Then the clubs started closing up—city noise ordinances, thinly veiled concessions to the white yuppies moving back into the inner city—and at the same time hip-hop groups and DJs were snapping up what little work was left. The crowds started treating Living Soul like a wedding band, making requests, asking for Top 40 hits. His bandmates began to drop off, and he had to hire jobbers, slick cats who showed up late and left as soon as the set was over. It wasn't worth it anymore. Asa Fern had come up singing in the church, and at age thirty-three, he went limping back.

"They played me a recording they made," the Reverend was saying. "Very poor sound quality, but they came across as talented, dedicated."

The Reverend was already in love with the idea of helping the kids record. But the man wasn't bothered with details. What did he know about talent? For all the musicality in his preaching, the Reverend had terrible taste, lite FM and smooth jazz: Ramsey Lewis, Grover Washington, and—unthinkable, unpardonable, unholy—Kenny G.

As he was preparing to go home, there was a knock on his door. Bella stood before him, penitent and truculent all at once. "Come on," Mr. Fern said, "get it out already."

"I just wanted to say . . . sorry about your wife, about what I said the other day."

"Damn right you're sorry, now you want to get your little album made."

"Aw, man . . ." She hadn't expected this. She'd expected to be indulged. "I don't know your wife, Mr. Fern."

"No, you don't."

"So, it ain't nothing personal."

"Nothing personal against *her*, you mean."

"I was just trying to make them laugh, you know how it is. Someone goes one up, so then you got to go higher than them. It's freestyle, we don't mean nothing by it. It's how we keep our skills sharp." Was this her idea of being contrite? "I guess it was kinda cheap, what I said. I should be better than that." She seemed more concerned with her reputation than his feelings. "We want to speak about the higher things, Mr. Fern."

"Holy hip-hop, is that it?"

"Nah, man, don't put a label on it. That's how they all do: Put a label on it, dismiss it, talk shit about it—" He raised his eyebrows. "Pardon me," she said.

She was covering her tracks. They didn't want to make Christian music. Apostles was a good name, and they figured they could get the Reverend behind them if they connected their efforts to the church. Mr. Fern almost smiled. He remembered how hard he used to hustle to get Living Soul gigs.

She handed him a tape—a cassette tape!

"Don't you own one of those iThings, whatever they're called?"

"Ty's older brother got a computer, but it's like twenty years old."

Mr. Fern put the tape in his player. Under the hiss, a simple descending line played on an out-of-tune piano, the battered old upright in the church basement, he suspected. Someone beat-boxed. They were too close to the microphone, and the drum noises blew out into distortion. And then, tiny and tinny, Bella's voice, rapping—*the baddest... the illest... streets of North Lawndale... but I never tire*—a sharp, wheedling voice, agile and cutting. He stopped the tape. Bella looked at him expectantly.

"It sounds terrible. You can hardly make out the words. It sounds like it was recorded underwater."

He wanted to wound her the way she'd wounded him. She didn't even blink. Jesus, how was he going to get rid of her?

"Here." He opened the bottom drawer of his desk and took out his portable four-track recorder. It was still in its original box, along with the upgraded external mic. He'd used it to record the choir several years ago for a contest. They didn't even accept submissions on tape anymore. "You can take this."

"We already got a tape, and it sounds like . . . crap."

"That's consumer-grade. This is professional." He took it out of the box and adjusted its settings. "This was state-of-the-art. This thing—" he tapped the four-track lovingly—"was built to last."

She looked skeptical but seized the machine anyway. "Ty gonna love this. He does the beats and the samples. He's my producer."

Over the next couple weeks, the four-track went everywhere with them. Mr. Fern saw them on the church steps, beat-boxing and rapping into it. Out in the neighborhood, Ty skulked around with the unit slung over his shoulder, wearing a pair of earmuff-sized headphones, pointing the microphone at anything that moved. He was an odd kid, fastidious and a little soft. Small for his age with a small, bullet-shaped head, he seemed to come and go without anyone paying him notice. He recorded little kids playing four square, women gossiping in the nail shop, the old Korean man who ran the corner store on Pulaski and Sixteenth telling rambling stories about how the neighborhood used to be. Down the block, the self-styled gangsters sat in their Cadillac, their car stereo quaking out bass. Ty snuck up behind them, crouched down, pointed the mic at the rattling trunk. This last one was clever, Mr. Fern thought: Bella would rap over that beat, so distorted and bloated on the low end it was practically a different rhythm. One Sunday, during the sermon, Mr. Fern looked over at Ty. The tambourine hung at his side, and the microphone peeked out from under his robe, to record the Reverend preaching.

Bella went everywhere with her head down and her brow furrowed, muttering to herself, stopping to write something on a crumpled sheet of notepaper, sometimes angrily scratching it out. As he passed the door to the church basement, Mr. Fern heard Marshall plinking away at the piano. The weather had gotten cold these last few weeks, but all summer Mr. Fern had seen Marshall on the basketball court or chasing around on his bike; strange now to have him hiding down in the basement, making minute changes to the same repetitive melodies. Marshall's lines wandered in and out of keys, never finding a proper tonal center, but in idle moments, Mr. Fern found himself humming them. He almost went down and told Marshall to quit; that out-of-tune piano was driving him crazy. But he held off. He hardly believed it—they were actually practicing.

"I don't want to get their hopes up," he told Regina one night. "None of this is a life skill, after all. They shouldn't get too hung up on it."

"Oh, they'll have some nice memories. Even if nothing comes from it."

She was right, but even as she said it, he scorned the thought. She was too complacent. All that money her family spent sending her to Oberlin—she could've been a concert pianist, an accompanist at the least. After the accident, she gave up on having a performance career. On a certain level, he understood. It hadn't just been the loss of her leg; she'd needed months of therapy before her motor functions came fully back. And he knew she liked her job in the showroom, helping other people find their perfect instrument. Still, she could've persevered. He often felt that her idleness had infected him, caused him to give up too early on his own career. At the same time, he'd wanted to provide for her, to protect her; he would've done whatever he thought she desired.

"If you start something," he said with sudden violence, "you're a damn fool if you don't see it through."

Regina put down the shirt she was folding, looked at him questioningly. "All right, then. I wasn't arguing with you."

———————

Soft, too-careful footsteps passing his office door made Mr. Fern pause in making notes on a score. He opened the door and caught Ty in the hallway, twenty minutes early for rehearsal. "Come on in here," Mr. Fern called out. Ty wore a stocking cap, pulled low over his brow. It didn't conceal anything; he carried his whole body stiffly. "Let me see," Mr. Fern said. Ty took off the cap, stared at the ground. "Look at me." He had a black eye and a welt across his forehead. The eye was closing up.

"Tyler," Mr. Fern began, like a scolding mother.

"Motherfuckers," Ty said between gritted teeth, his voice gone suddenly husky, "those thieving-ass motherfuckers." He'd gone back to record the older boys sitting in their Cadillac. When they saw what he was doing, they pushed him around, took away the four-track and all the tapes, then gave him a beating.

Mr. Fern gently touched the skin around the welt. He went to the kitchen and came back with an ice pack wrapped in a towel. In the hallway, he pressed it against his own forehead, feeling a headache coming on. More than anything, he was annoyed about losing the machine.

Ty winced against the ice pack. "All that work, gone," he said. His lip began to quiver, and then he broke into tears. Mr. Fern wiped them roughly away with the corner of the towel.

"You haven't lost hardly anything. It took near six months to record my first album."

It turned out to be the right thing to say. Ty was curious. "Oh, yeah? What'd you record it on?" He almost took the bait. Instead he sent Ty home. "Your grandma there?" Ty nodded yes. "Well, get on, then."

In rehearsal, Bella and Marshall looked for Ty, but Mr. Fern didn't have the heart to tell them what had happened.

He was halfway home when he saw the Cadillac parked on the corner of Lawndale and Nineteenth. Three boys leaned against it, drinking beer. Bass pulsed the air around them, the trunk vibrating with each note. He stared right at them, but they paid him no notice. He went over. This was dumb. On every level this was dumb.

One of the boys was older than the others, taller and more muscular. Mr. Fern took stock of him. He was handsome, arrogant, a little bored just hanging around with his two buddies. He posed as he leaned against the car, maybe hoping some girls would come by. But there was too much self-consciousness about him. His Air Jordans were scuffed at the toes and his red satin Bulls jacket frayed at the cuffs; he was embarrassed to present himself in last season's clothes. Mr. Fern knew what everyone in the neighborhood knew: For a year or more, these boys had been losing a turf war over the traffic on the west side. These days, no one came to them for anything.

Mr. Fern spoke: ". . . down." He tried again: ". . . it down!" Finally he shouted, "Turn that goddamn noise down!" A long, lazy moment passed before the kid in the Jordans reached into the car and dialed down the volume. The three of them stood staring. *What the fuck you want, old man?*

"You all proud of yourselves, stealing from a little kid?" The two younger boys smiled at each other. The music was still loud. The bass filled his head, made it difficult to string the words together. "Listen, I want you to give me those tapes back."

"Why you think we gonna do that?" the oldest boy finally said. He didn't even bother to deny they had them.

Mr. Fern closed his eyes and choked back a shout. It was a boy like this—he had no way of knowing, and yet he believed it without a doubt—who had knocked Regina down that day, who'd sped off, drunk and scared, and left her lying broken on the asphalt.

"Listen, you keep that recorder." *Listen*, why did he keep saying *listen*? "But try selling it through some dumb-ass hype, see what you get for it. Now if I *tell* you where to go, you'll get five hundred. That thing's vintage, you hardly see that model anymore. But not too many people going to be interested. You need a specialist."

"So, tell us already."

"You give me those tapes first. They're not worth anything."

"Yeah, I get it. You tell us where to go, and then you call that thing in stolen. Think we're stupid or something."

"I think that if I try and get y'all arrested, you're going to repay that on me—you're going to start hanging around, make my life a misery. Hell, you got nothing better to do than bring your misery around this neighborhood." He knew he was going too far now, but he couldn't help it. He was furious. "What use you got for those tapes anyhow? Can't play them on nothing."

One of the younger boys said, "Think we want to listen to some bullshit anyway?" The other, recognizing him from somewhere: "Hey, you the guy who works over at the ice rink?"

The oldest boy reached into the back seat. "Here." He tossed the three tapes in Mr. Fern's direction. He managed to catch two, the third clattered on the ground.

"Go downtown, to Azarello's. Tell them you found this in an antique store or something, I don't know. Tell them the previous owner cared for it, *maintained* it."

They all laughed at him now. "Shit," the oldest boy said, "he's in love with this piece of shit."

At home, he put on one of the tapes. It was better. It wasn't great. They hadn't quite figured out how to line up the tracks. Ty's samples were out of time. Marshall's ideas on piano were beyond him technically; he only seemed to feel comfortable in C and G major but kept moving out of those keys, hearing something denser and more complex but not knowing how to translate it to the keyboard. Bella's rapping was steady and more rhythmically sophisticated than he'd expected, but her voice was mixed too low and the other sounds were canceling it out. He got a beer from the fridge and listened to half of the second tape and part of the third. Reverend Williams's voice repeated on a loop—"The Apostles were students, the Apostles were messengers"—while Bella rapped about how good a rapper she was. He ejected the tape and put it with the others next to his car keys, intending to take them to church with him on Sunday. But then he thought better of it and instead hid them out of sight in a drawer.

In the kitchen, he made up a tray of chocolate chip cookies and milk. He took it down to them, but they hardly touched it—they weren't here on a play date; this was serious work. A pile of blouses hung over the back of an old La-Z-Boy. Regina came down here to do her ironing and listen to old musicals. Mr. Fern flipped on the lights in the corner of the room he'd used as his studio. It seemed meager now: a Fostek half-inch tape machine, a mixing board, a pair of bulky speakers for monitoring, a gut-string acoustic guitar, a few small percussion toys. There'd once been an entire drum set and several guitar amplifiers down here. He'd sold them off over the years to pay household bills.

The remainder of his equipment sat on high shelves he'd built to keep things dry in case the basement flooded. Ty was already dragging down the drum machine, an original Roland 808, a bulky black box crowded with tiny knobs and switches. "Never had much use for this thing," Mr. Fern said as he hooked it up. "They said it was going to be the future, but listen to it." He tapped a few of the buttons: a tinny, white-noise snare drum, a ridiculously low-pitched bass drum, a hand clap. Ty's eyes went wide. He hunched over the machine, crowding Mr. Fern out, and started turning knobs and changing settings — amazing how quickly he picked it up. "Ill," he murmured as the machine emitted various noises, "this is too ill." Within a few minutes, he'd worked out an entire drumbeat, snare, bass drum, and high-hat stuttering away. "That's older than old school," he announced. "Listen up, y'all, cause that's a history lesson right there."

"All right, all right" — Mr. Fern paused the machine — "that thing gets on my nerves."

"Let's record one of our songs," Bella said. "Let's do 'Fresh till Death'!"

Mr. Fern pretended to consider it, critically tapping his chin with his index finger, then pretended to change his mind. "Why don't we work on something new, start from scratch, see what happens? That's the way I always work best. Element of surprise. Okay, we got drums, now we need a bass line."

He took down his Minimoog synthesizer. Down at the bottom of the keyboard, he played a few squelchy, syncopated bass figures. "Whoa!" Bella said, only half-sarcastically. "Hold on, Mr. Fern getting funky."

"A little less," Marshall said, leaning over the keyboard. "Yeah, a little sparser." He made a tamping down motion with his hand. "Make it cold, RZA-style. Yeah, dope."

Mr. Fern shook his head in disbelief. Here he was, taking direction from a thirteen-year-old. "Okay," he said, "we got drums, we got bass. Let's lay something down." He reached over and set the tape machine whirring, pushed start on the 808, and then, after eight bars, played his keyboard part over the drums.

Bella was already poring over her crumpled sheets of notepaper, her ashy lips moving silently as she mouthed her lyrics. "I can get down on this," she said as they listened back to the tracks. "I can get right down on this."

"Here," Mr. Fern said, hooking up a microphone and placing it in front of her. It was a big, tube-driven mic in a heavy steel casing — besides Regina's wedding ring, the most expensive, significant thing he'd ever bought. "No, don't hold it. You're not onstage yet. If you hold it, you get all kinds of noise. Just go with whatever comes to mind," he said, softening a little. "Don't overthink it." Bella gave him a pitying look that said, I've practiced this, don't tell me to just wing it. He hooked up a pair of headphones. She wore them with only one earpiece pressed to her head, something she must have learned from music videos. One hand chopped the air as she rapped:

> Beauty only skin deep
> Beauty as in *Bella*
> See me on the streets
> Won't see me in the cellar
> Born in '91, they say that was a good year
> But, shit, I never tire
> Apostles set the block on fire
> Daddy said I was a mistake
> Mama said he was a liar

"Good," Mr. Fern said, stopping the tape. "Do it again."

She looked at him. *Are you crazy? That was perfect.* Finally, he'd hurt her. She was proud of this talent. She might make something of herself if she kept it up, if someone didn't come along and stamp out that proud fire too soon. "It was good," he explained, "but your rhythm was off in places. What?" he said, pushing her a little. "Think you'd get it first take? You want to do it right, don't you?"

She nodded yes.

"Also, if you're going to take the Reverend's money, no cussing."

They ran it twice more. He played it back. "Sounds better, right?"

"Yeah," she said grudgingly.

"Okay, that's our scratch track. Vocals always come last." He paused, held her gaze. "Final vocals always come last. Nothing's more important." He turned to Marshall. "We need a hook. Got anything?"

Marshall played a few tentative melody lines on the Minimoog. "Up an octave," Mr. Fern prompted. "Good, now a little less." He smiled slyly. "And here, remember the key. We're in A minor. You remember I taught y'all that scale, right?" Marshall played a nice, simple ornament around the fifth. "Good, good. That last note, take it up a half step."

"But it sounds dope, man."

"It clashes with the bass line. It makes a tritone." He played the dissonant interval. "*Diabolus in musica*. The devil in music." He smiled again. "Okay, play it over the other tracks." He started up the tape machine again. "No, no, don't play every measure. Save it till the end of the phrase."

"But it's the best part," Marshall said.

"And that's why you hold it back. Give them just a little. Keep them coming back just to hear that one moment. It creates an illusion."

"Illusion of what?" Marshall said.

"That you got a million of these ideas lined up and waiting in the wings."

He was about to say more when he heard the basement door open. "Asa?" Regina called down.

"Baby, we're working on our album."

"Asa, you'd better come upstairs." Something in her voice kept him from protesting again.

She was just home from work. She still had her jacket on. "What, what is it?" he said, following her through the kitchen and down the front steps. He went down to the car. There were big dents in the hood, and gang tags had been keyed onto the side panels. Three windows had been smashed. On the front seat, the four-track sat in a pile of glass.

"Didn't you hear anything?"

"I was downstairs."

"They didn't even take anything. They just left that machine."

He hadn't told her about getting the tapes back. He didn't want her to worry. She took a step back, wobbled on her leg. He caught her, held her tight. She was trembling.

"Let's go inside," he said, "I'll call the police."

When he went back downstairs, Bella, Ty, and Marshall knew something was wrong. They sensed it had to do with them. He stood there, not knowing what to say.

"Listen," Ty said. They'd already added another verse to the song. "It was nothing to figure out how to work the tape machine," Ty bragged.

"Now all we need is a chorus" — Marshall played another melody on the keyboard — "something like this."

Bella was putting the microphone in front of him, handing him a piece of paper with lyrics scratched out on it. He looked at it, bewildered.

"Come on, Mr. Fern," she said. "Sing."

The
Bridge

———————

When Kate brought her mom in from her nap, the rest of us—me, Kate's dad, her two brothers—couldn't help but stare. It was the first we'd seen of the new wig.

"Finally," Kate's mom said as Kate got her settled at the table, "the first meal on the veranda."

It was late April, and we were sitting in wicker chairs at the long wicker table looking out over the lake. The food—roast duck, fried polenta, a whole tray of glistening asparagus—had arrived twenty minutes earlier, and Kate's dad had paid the caterer extra to serve it up for us. We sat with squares of paper towel in our laps (no one could find the cloth napkins) waiting to eat, our wine glasses already full.

"Good nap, Mom?" Cooper, Kate's older brother, said. She didn't answer him. "Good rest, Mom?" he said more loudly, as if she were deaf. He wasn't looking her in the eyes but a little higher.

It was a deep strawberry color with flashes of orange underneath, and it shone wetly in the outside spotlighting that made it feel like we were on a stage. The wig was meant to be glamorous, like it had been chopped and styled in a fancy salon. The top and sides were flared up like one of those lizards preparing for combat. I hadn't seen Kate's mom for maybe a month. Her face had puffed up. She had on a billowy ochre dress with long sleeves, and underneath her body seemed to have collapsed into strange, lumpy shapes. That was the steroid medication. She wasn't underweight anyway.

Kate sat down between me and her mom. She touched my knee under the table. *Act natural*, that touch said.

Kate's mom turned to regard Cooper. He wore pressed khakis and a yellow Ralph Lauren button down.

"Nice rest?" she said weakly. "Yes. Thank you."

For a moment, the two of them sat there looking like they'd never seen each other in this world and were trying not to betray the fact.

"This looks delicious, everyone," Kate's dad said.

"The first meal on the veranda," Cooper repeated grandly. It was their family tradition to open up the screened porch at the back of the house with a big summer meal. It wasn't quite the first nice day of the year—late April in Michigan wasn't exactly summer—but close enough. "It all looks great," Cooper went on. "Really great."

"Enough ceremony," Kate's dad said. "Eat."

We heaped it up on our plates. I hadn't stopped for anything on the drive from Chicago, and I wasn't going to let Kate's dad or Cooper edge me out. Eldridge, Kate's middle brother, was a picker. He served himself half a slice of polenta. He didn't like much of anything.

For a few minutes, it was just knives and forks clinking plates. A breeze blowing up from the lake was *shushing* the willow that hung over the corner of the house. We could hear the waves and a buoy farther out making gulping sounds. Kate finished cutting up her mom's food and started in on her own. I wondered what was going through all of their heads. The same doctors who said cutting a chunk out of Mom's brain and irradiating the rest would give her another year were now saying, More like two months.

"When we did this last year there was still ice on the lake," Cooper said, directing a smile at each of us as if he were addressing a conference.

"Well, I remember taking the boat out," Eldridge said drily. "I remember it pretty clearly. We caught some perch."

Kate gave both of them a look, an expression on her face I could only describe as vigilant. "I think he's right, Coop," she said.

"Gas is cheap up here," I said out of nowhere. Now that Kate had spoken, I felt I could too. "Remember when it was three bucks a gallon? Wish I could fill up double before I go back down."

Actually, I barely had enough in my wallet to get back to Chicago. Cooper lived in Cincinnati—wife, two boys, midlevel management in some big insurance company. Eldridge had flown in from Key West, where he busied himself with partying and sponging off his dad. Kate had taken it on herself to drive up from the city to take care of her mom—four or five days of every week for the last three months. She'd lost track of her friends, all but quit her job downtown. We'd been living off my cocktail gigs. I'd had to call a drummer friend to sub on two of them just to get out of the city that weekend.

"We've been looking at those hybrids," Kate's dad said to me.

"You bet," I said. I didn't know a thing about them. "Pretty tempting."

That kind of talk went on for a few minutes and ended with Cooper asserting that he too was in the market for a hybrid auto. Eldridge said that he just read in a magazine that one of four hybrid owners also had an SUV in the garage, knowing very well how proud Cooper had been to show off his new Chevy Tahoe that Christmas.

"Times change," Cooper said peevishly. "Needs change." Eldridge was only teasing—anyone could tell—but his older brother would never hear it that way.

Cooper turned to his mother again. "What do you think, Mom?" he said. "Should *any* of us get a new car?"

From the end of the table, she stared back at us. She hadn't eaten more than a bite or two. Her face had gone slack, but there was a kind of haughtiness lighting her eyes. For a moment, I had the distinct impression that she was holding court with us.

"I'd like some of that, please," she said to no one in particular, pointing at the gravy boat. We passed it down. She curlicued gravy over her duck and asparagus, then returned the gravy boat to its saucer and sat with her hands folded in her lap.

"Would you like anything else, Mom?" Kate said carefully, deliberately.

We'd all stopped eating. Everything seemed to have come to a halt. By the measured tone of Kate's voice, I understood that this was one of her mother's slips: She got confused sometimes; things didn't quite link up. On a good day, one of the doctors had said, she was about seventy, eighty percent her old self. The week before, she'd thought there were crows in the house, and she'd opened all the windows wide and run the vacuum and the blender on full power to scare them out. You had to wait, Kate said, and trust that in a few minutes, or after a little rest, she would come back.

"Mom?" Cooper said. "Can we — "

She just looked at him and he quit talking.

"Excuse me," she said, "but is the musician here yet?"

Kate laughed. We all laughed. It was maybe a little cruel, but it was better to keep things light. Actually, that Kate's mom had spoken at all was a relief.

"You mean Tim, Mom," Kate said. She reached over and wiped a spot of gravy off her mother's blouse. "He's right here. He arrived when you were napping."

Kate's mom looked at me. She made a sweeping gesture with her hand. "I'm ready," she said. "Please go ahead."

I sat there doing my best to smile. Her eyes had emptied out. There wasn't even a dot of recognition in them. I can say it more easily now, from a distance, but it's true that I never held much affection for Kate's mother. She hadn't been a fan of mine either. She was protective of her husband's money and had always suspected I'd just try to become another sponge like Eldridge. When the diagnosis came, I'd felt it would be wrong to work up some kind of great, false sympathy for the entire family. When you try to throw yourself into other people's suffering, I thought then, you end up making it all seem like a trinket—flashy, cheap and tasteless. I was there that weekend to support Kate.

"Mom, he's not going to sing a song or anything," Kate said.

"No, Katherine, the violin." As if it was obvious.

"Tim is a percussionist, Mom."

"It's Kate's boyfriend," Cooper put in. I always hated the way he said *boyfriend*, a reminder that, after three years, Kate and I living together two of them, I was still only that to her family. "He's a drummer, Mom," Cooper added.

"When the other musicians arrive," Kate's mom said, "tell them to start right away."

She wasn't getting her way. She didn't understand why there wasn't already a string quartet sawing away in her backyard.

"Why don't you sing something, Tim?" Kate said gently. "Sing an old jazz song."

"What songs do you know?" Kate's dad asked me.

"I know about a thousand," I said. Serious jazz musicians know anywhere from two to three thousand. At that time, I considered myself well on the way to serious. "I don't know the lyrics to all of them."

Kate's mom was staring at me. Those eyes were like looking at the sky on a clear day and realizing there's nothing up there but space and more space. I sat looking at her puffed-up face and the flame-colored spume of woven horsehair sitting on top of it, and I couldn't think of one song I'd even heard, let alone sung or played.

To hesitate is to lose, my own father once said. He wrote it in a letter to me when I was seventeen, a grand letter full of grand advice, just before he left to go out to Oregon to sell personal computers door-to-door, back when people still thought you could succeed at such things. Actually, he wrote, "To hesitate is to loose." He was ignorant, and that was only one of the reasons I didn't miss him much. Since, I have often wondered if he wasn't right both ways.

I sat there with my palms sweating, starting to feel embarrassed, and then irritated that I should have to feel embarrassed. If I'd just broken out into song, we all could have laughed. It wouldn't have had to be more than a few bars. But, then, we were all just acting, pretending that a song would suddenly make everything right again, that it would bring Kate's mother back from whatever strange tracks her mind had shunted onto.

"What's that one you always liked, Mom?" Kate said. "That Sarah Vaughn song?" And then Kate started singing "If I Were a Bell"—sweetly, but off-key. After a few bars, I joined in behind her.

The waves went on murmuring and the buoy gulping, and Kate and I sounded small and helpless, singing out against the tremendous quiet of the evening. Kate's mom had gone stiff, her whole body. Her mouth was gaping, and she'd rocked herself up on her hands so that she leaned over the table like a ski jumper. She started making a low, humming noise to herself—more a gargle than a tune. Kate and I trailed off midverse.

"Mom," Kate said, "how about a piece of Black Forest cake?"

She didn't answer. She was still midair in her ski jump.

"Let's finish our dinners," Kate said after a moment. "Come on, don't let it go to waste."

We took up knives and forks again. This was where we waited it out.

"The duck is superb," Cooper tried to say casually, or like he was being slowly strangled.

Eldridge agreed. He said he couldn't wait to try the cake. I didn't know if there really was one, but I said how much I'd like a slice too. I went on eating, not tasting a thing. And after a few minutes, she did come back. She relaxed into her chair, then sat looking dazed and upset. We asked if she was all right, but she couldn't seem to get her tongue around any words. She stared down at her plate. Kate cut up a few more bites of food for her, but she wouldn't eat.

While the rest of us cleared the table, Kate got her mom set up in bed. Eldridge, Cooper, and I did the dishes. We looked at each other solemnly, saying almost nothing—as if we had much to talk about anyway—like scraping a plate into the garbage disposal or putting slices of duck meat into Tupperware containers was of great, ritual significance to us. We could hear the TV playing the local news in the bedroom. It was a report on a hot-air balloon race.

In those days, Kate and I knew how to find each other instinctively.

After we finished clearing up, I slipped down to the lake. There was an old tree stump with a little bench notched into it where you could sit and look across the water. I thought I'd escaped for a few minutes. I wasn't surprised when I heard footsteps padding down through the grass.

Eldridge sat down beside me.

"You're in my spot," he said. From his pocket, he brought out a pipe—one of his father's—struck a match, and began to puff on some very sweet-smelling tobacco. "That was a real circus at dinner, huh?"

Eldridge was maybe a year or two younger than I was. He was tall and tanned and good-looking and charming without ever really trying. He was also easy to ignore. He smoked his father's pipe, I sat listening to the waves. Every few minutes, I could hear the almost silent popping of largemouth bass rising to the surface.

"This family is pretty close," Eldridge said. "Might not seem like it, I know. Cooper and I, we're the worst." He laughed to himself. "Guess I beat him up one too many times when we were kids." He tilted back his head and tried to blow a couple of smoke rings. "Kate's been pretty great about all of this, I'll say that much."

If he was trying to have a heart-to-heart with me, it wasn't working. Maybe he was apologizing for what had happened at dinner, or he wanted me to feel comfortable speaking my mind. All I could think was that while he was down in Florida living free, I hadn't made love to Kate in almost five weeks.

"We're all wrapped up pretty tight in this," he went on. "It can be kind of suffocating. But it's the kind of thing that brings people together."

He was saying it, but I don't think he believed a word. It sounded like he was reading off the back of a cereal box.

"What kind of tobacco is that?"

"Apple flavored. I got it for my dad for his birthday a few years ago. Never got smoked. Not till now anyway."

"I'm sorry."

"It's okay," Eldridge said. "He just likes his regular tobacco."

"That wig is something."

"I kind of like it."

"Sure. Me too."

After a while, Eldridge took the pipe out of his mouth and knocked the remaining tobacco out onto the grass. "Tastes terrible," he said. He stood, gave me a chuck on the shoulder, and went back up to the house.

After a few minutes, I got up and followed him. Halfway up the lawn, I stopped. I walked back down to the lake, this time veering over to the far side of the property, where there was a little strip of sand that Kate's family called their private beach. The sky was clear. There was a sliver of moon. The little lampposts running along the shore path were baubles in the thick, sultry dusk.

"There you are."

I could just see her in silhouette. She was in the water, her jeans rolled up, the waves slowly washing in coming up to her knees.

"You look like a wild woman, Kate."

"It's nice out." Her voice floated up to me. "I couldn't help dipping my toes in." She trailed her hands in the water. After a quiet moment she said, "Want to come in?"

I left my shoes and socks in the grass, rolled up the cuffs of my trousers. The bottom was rocky. I picked my way out to her. We stood together looking back at the shore and the lights along the path and the lights of the houses. The water was freezing.

"Cold knees," I said.

"Cold feet," she said.

I should have just reached out and held her.

"Where'd you get the hairpiece?'

"There's a place in Ann Arbor. It's something, isn't it? You could have used it back in your heavy metal days."

"I felt like a wandering minstrel in there."

"Did we get the words right? I haven't heard that song in years."

"Is she going to wear it out in public?"

We looked at each other in the faint light of the moon. All around us I could hear the popping of fish coming to the surface. "Cooper asked too. We've still got the old wig. Maybe I can talk her into it—new wig for at home, old wig for going out."

The wind blew up and fanned Kate's hair across her face. She brushed it away, then brought what must have been a hair tie out of her pocket and pulled her hair back into a ponytail.

"I'm not sure how many of these weekends I have left in the checking account."

She seemed annoyed that I kept bringing up money. "We don't have to worry about that." I didn't know what I found more offensive—that I would borrow money from her father, or that she would get it for me.

"Come home. Just for a week. You need a break."

She didn't answer me. A man was passing by on the shore path walking a big, white Akita. The dog shone out through the dark. The man stopped and stood staring at us, trying to make out what we were doing.

"Haven't put the pier in yet!" Kate called out. Her dad hadn't gotten around to contacting the service. Other things on his mind. The man waved to us. "Hi, there," he called back, as if he hadn't heard Kate speak. He thought we were trespassing. He looked around him like he should be calling for help. After a minute, he whistled to his dog and continued down the shore path. The Akita floated along in the dark like a lantern. I looked down at Kate's hands. The whole time they'd been churning up the water around her.

"Is there really cake?" I said.

"I made that up. I'll find you something else. There's enough food in the house."

We sloshed our way back to the shore and in our bare feet walked silently up through the grass.

———

Just before bed I joined Kate's dad for a nightcap. If Kate's dad and I had a ritual, drinking his expensive scotch out on the front steps was it. He brought out a bottle of Talisker, poured my glass to the brim. All Kate's dad knew how to do was offer people things, say try this, and this. Why don't you have some more? No, go ahead. Help yourself.

"Plenty of earth and ocean in this bottle." He took a sip. "Peaty," he said.

When it went down it went right down. Started a little fire in my belly and made a hot, wide-open space in the front of my skull.

"Tastes like a good one," I said.

Kate's parents lived at the end of a private road, and all we could see from the porch were the dark outlines of the other big houses squatting in among the trees. I wondered if it gave Kate's dad any real pride to own the largest of these houses, to live at the end of such an exclusive road. Or was it just another thing he had simply expected—to settle into permanent comfort by the time he was forty, raise a family on the beautiful shore of a lake, and summon them back every Easter, Thanksgiving, and Christmas, for long weekends, birthdays, the first meal out on the veranda? And then he would retire peacefully into even greater comfort. A perfect life, in the end—but for the fact that his wife had just been lobotomized and she'd be dead by the middle of summer. I sipped my scotch and I sat thinking all of that. And I got very gloomy despite the good whisky and thought that I was a cruel son of a bitch for feeling that misfortune should be visited equally on the heads of everyone, even the rich. Even Kate's family.

I started to ask for another glass. Just then the screen door swung open and Cooper came out, and almost immediately he started talking about his older son. He'd spoken to his wife on the phone—James had just done his first night as the lead, as Tom Sawyer, in the school musical. Cooper told us that he'd attended the dress rehearsal and that all the teachers involved were praising little James to the moon. The strange thing about Cooper was his hair. No matter how much stuff he put on it he couldn't get his cowlick to stay down. He sat there, talking away, and every minute or so, he'd reach up and smooth the thing down. It kept popping back up. He looked like Astro Boy.

When Cooper finished, his dad tipped back his glass and drained the last of his scotch. He cleared his throat. He looked out into the woods, wiped his mouth with the back of his hand.

"Tell Pauline to send us some pictures" was all he said.

Cooper stood looking at his father on the step, a big grin frozen on his face, his eyes shining. "No problem, Dad," he murmured. "No problem."

From across the lawn, we heard the quick electric snap of the bug light. I counted six bugs meeting their end.

"Do they whitewash the fence?" I said.

Cooper looked at me like I had just materialized out of thin air.

"What?"

"The fence. Do they do the whitewashing scene? It's *Tom Sawyer*, right?"

"Of course," he said. "They even use real paint." He laughed a high laugh. "With all their rehearsals, they must have painted it fifty times already."

It seemed to me that they wouldn't have gone to all that trouble, that the kids would have just mimed it in rehearsal. Cooper was exaggerating, trying to impress his father. I wasn't going to let the air out of him.

"What kind of paint do they use?"

"Well, I don't know," Cooper said philosophically. "Latex? House paint? Whatever whitewash is."

"It's just cheap stuff," I said. "It's anything."

"Anything," Cooper agreed. "Just any old paint, I guess."

Kate's dad grunted. He put his tumbler on the porch railing, stood up. "I need to check on your mother."

He left Cooper and me out on the front steps. That was the end of our conversation, I thought. "Might turn in," I said. "Pretty long day."

Cooper picked up the tumbler his dad had just put down between his thumb and forefinger, as if it were a hazardous object.

"Do you ever zone out, Tim?" he said, almost savagely.

"Sorry?"

"I used to play the electric guitar. You didn't know that, did you?"

"I didn't."

"When I played I used to zone out. I'd forget all about what time it was. I'd even miss dinner. Mom encouraged me, said she liked hearing me play." He reached up and tried to smooth down his cowlick. It stuck up like an aerial. "Yes, sir, the electric guitar. I gave it up. I didn't think it was a serious thing to do."

I didn't know if he was insulting me or baring his soul. Poor Cooper, he never found the right tone in anything.

"It isn't serious at all," I said. "That's what makes it fun."

A rueful smile came across his face. "Sure," he said. "Sure. How could I miss that?" He looked exhausted. Whatever he'd been pushing for his entire life, he couldn't even win it while his mother was dying. Underneath the starched khakis and the pressed polo, the twelve-year-old boy was still desperately trying to learn all the scales on his electric guitar.

"Get some sleep," I told him. "We all need a little."

When I got into bed with Kate, I felt like I'd been swimming against a strong current all day, like I'd traveled a great distance without getting anywhere at all. She had her reading glasses on. A *National Geographic* rested beside her on the sheets. The cover read, "Beluga Whales."

I lay there looking at her in the light of the bedside lamp — her dusky blond hair, high cheekbones, freckles — and I thought that when I was alone again in Chicago I wouldn't even be able to picture her face. It made me nauseated to be reminded how beautiful she was. When we were first dating she seemed as haughty as her mother. I didn't understand then how I could be falling in love with a rich girl. Well, if she'd grown up with Cooper and Eldridge and managed to stay sane, there must have been something special about her.

"Your brothers have been baring their souls to me," I said. "It's been exhausting."

"They think you're cool," she said.

"Cooper thinks I'm cool?"

"He said so."

My fingers had been searching under the blankets. They found the waistband of Kate's panties.

"Jesus," I said, "really? *Cooper*?"

"Weren't we just fighting?"

"Were we? I can't tell. I can't tell anymore."

She let out a long sigh. "I'm just glad you came this weekend. I'm starting to lose my mind. I couldn't take it without you here."

"Me too."

And then Kate and I did each other with fingers and hands.

Too quiet in that house to do it all. Too still. We were sweating down in that basement. I caught mine in a Kleenex, crept upstairs afterward to flush it. We lay on top of the sheets.

"Long day," I began. "The longest. We need sleep."

I turned to her. She already was.

Usually, lying in that plush bed, listening to the waves muttering at the lakeshore, I slept like a drowned man. That night I woke around two, and I felt without doubt or hesitation that there was someone in the house. Kate's dad had their place alarmed better than most banks, but in all the confusion of the day, we must have forgotten to lock up the veranda.

I crept upstairs and in my socks shuffled through the kitchen and the high-vaulted living room to the rear of the house. I went out to the veranda—sure enough, the door was unlocked—and I sat in the dark in the same wicker chair I'd had at dinner. I sat waiting for whoever I thought it was had broken into Kate's parents' house. I wasn't sure what I'd do. Maybe I'd just scare him enough he'd run for it.

After sitting there a few minutes, thinking confused, sleep-ridden thoughts, I satisfied myself it was only my imagination. It had been a night for false, wayward signals. I poked my head into a few dark rooms, the pantry, the home office, looked behind the shower curtain in the bathroom, and then I went back down and got into bed. It was chilly now. I carefully worked myself in under the covers.

And of course I didn't sleep at all. I stared at the ceiling. I listened to the waves. Kate hadn't had a decent night's sleep in days, and I tried to keep still. But when I heard the sound—a quiet, snuffling sound—I understood what had woken me in the first place.

It was coming from the laundry room just down the hall. I put on my socks again and closed the bedroom door behind me. The snuffling had stopped. I opened the slatted doors and saw a figure sprawled on the tile floor.

The fluorescent bulb blinked on. She was on her stomach, facing away from me, her nightgown hiked up to her thighs. The backs of her legs were crazed, all the way up, with dark purple and black veins. Behind her knees, she had big black bruises. All the weight she'd put on, those blood vessels were bursting like crazy. I could see, too, that she had on a pair of billowy lavender underpants.

"Angie," I whispered. It felt like I had never spoken her first name before. That might have been true. "Angie, you okay?"

The sleeve of her nightgown was bunched up in her mouth. She was biting down on it. She made the snuffling sound again. She was crying.

I knelt down next to her. I smoothed her hair. I didn't know what else to do. I got my hands underneath her armpits and managed to prop her up against the dryer. I rearranged her nightgown as best I could. She must have bitten her tongue. There was blood mixed up in the drool and it had run down her chin and stained the white piping on her nightgown.

"Jesus," I said out loud and immediately wished I hadn't. Maybe she hadn't understood. We met eyes. No, she was in there all right. She knew it was me.

"Angie," I said, "tell me you're okay."

My first thought was to run and get Kate. But I couldn't pull my eyes away. Crying, wetting, shitting yourself, someone who might as well be a stranger kneeling before you on a cold tile floor, wondering if he should wipe the drool off your chin — this, I knew, was the beginning of the end of these things. Not long until the professionals came in. They took away the real bed and replaced it with one that sat up for you. Then the sponge baths, the bed sores, the plastic bottle you had to pee in. And finally the morphine came, and it took away all the rest.

"I want to stand up."

"Maybe we should rest a while," I said.

"You're the expert." The words came out flat and expressionless. I realized that she was being sarcastic. "You're a musician," she said.

"I am."

"A drummer."

"Not much of a singer," I said.

I used the corner of my shirt to clean her up a little.

"What's the difference? Drummer? Percussionist?"

"I went to school for it."

"Tim," she said deliberately. A long moment passed. "Tim," she said, "Katherine's going to be married."

I wondered how much I had of her then. Seventy percent? Eighty? It didn't much matter. She was going to get what she wanted said one way or another.

"News to me, Angie," I tried to say lightly.

"Why not you?"

"I don't have a high opinion of the institution."

The blood had drained from her face. She was as pale and waxy as a turnip. She drew in a sharp breath. She burped. I realized two things at that moment: The washing machine was jiggling and humming behind us—it had just kicked onto spin cycle. And she was wearing her old wig, the mousy brown one.

"It needed a wash," she said.

I stood, opened the lid of the washing machine, and waited for the water to drain away. Big, wet hunks of strawberry red and orange hair were plastered to the sides of the cylinder. The main part was stuck to the bottom, looking like an animal carcass that had been dredged up from the lake.

"Everyone was staring at it."

I sat back down on the cold tile. Getting her back into bed would be difficult. I should get her wrapped up in something at least. I sat there wondering how any of this was going to be accomplished, and if I wanted to take it upon myself to risk it.

"Where do you go?" I said. "Where do you go off to when it happens?"

She didn't answer.

"You could tell me. I won't go spreading it around."

"It's called a seizure. It's nowhere. Why don't you make my daughter happy?"

And then it was my turn not to answer. A long, unhappy year later, things between Kate and me came to a bad end. I wouldn't let her give the engagement ring back. *Someday*, I kept telling her, full of stupid, false hope. *Someday you'll change your mind.* We were cut from different cloth, but that wasn't the reason things ended. I couldn't get it out of my head: Every time I remembered that night, it was a picture of Kate lying down there on the laundry room floor, not her mother.

"I want to stand up. Take me back to bed."

Always ordering people around. Some things don't change.

I got her under the armpits again and hefted her up. I expected her to stink. The smell was there, but it was covered by half a gallon of Chanel, the same stuff Kate used when we first met. By the time I got her to the top of the stairs, I was the one sweating. We paused in the living room so I could get my breath. When I started again, she wouldn't move.

"Come on," I said. "Keep going."

"No, listen."

I only heard the waves again. The waves and the willow and all the things that had accompanied me through the night. "Sure, I hear it," I lied.

"It's my song."

Not this again, I thought. I gave her a nudge forward, and we went on—her drooling, me huffing and grunting, the two of us clumsy-dancing to the music in her head.

"Listen," she said. "My song. My song."

Beginners

My father was never happy in work. His one great glory came when I was fourteen, about the time I started playing jazz seriously. He was a shift manager at the Interlaken Resort, a fancy hotel on the lake. He wore a mustache then, dyed and combed, and a sharply pressed pale yellow polo, and he wandered the carpeted halls of the complex with great purpose, straightening pictures, rearranging the continental breakfast, and playing grab-ass with the Mexican maids. He'd charmed his way in to the job; he didn't know a thing about hospitality. Somehow he lasted almost three years. They hated to let him go. Without being able to say what he actually did around the place, everyone seemed to love him.

A decade later, I had my first respectable gig, with the Charles Rigby Quintet. I was starting to play all around the city, starting to figure out how to make it pay. My father was living out in Florence, Oregon, where he worked in the loading bay of a Sam's Club, heaving around cases of frozen fish sticks, throwing himself into it like one of the boys. At fifty-two, his essential directionlessness had stranded him in cold storage. In this regard—direction, unswerving direction—our two separate lives had become nothing if not counterpoint.

Florence was the town where they had famously tried to unbeach the carcass of a beached whale using dynamite. When he went for walks by himself along the dunes, Dad swore he could still smell the charred blubber. He joked about it often. But I couldn't help thinking of him as the guy who would've cooked up the idea, the guy who, assuming a sensible and civic-minded expression, would've gleefully depressed the plunger.

"So, tell me, how's the musician's life?"

We talked every two weeks, noon on a Sunday, faithful to a schedule if nothing else.

"I've been sitting in with Chévere." I tried to keep my description simple. "It's this Afro-Cuban-fusion hit. Lots of mixed meter, clave in 7/8, kind of a late-seventies thing. Weather Report, Return to Forever, that kind of bag. But Latin-flavored."

"Uh huh," Dad said. "Uh huh, uh huh." I could almost see him nodding along, as if stirring up the brainpan would help him understand.

"The Charles Rigby group is gearing up to tour. I've been sheddin' like hell. Charles is finalizing the dates for Europe."

"Europe? The grand tour, huh? That's fantastic, really fantastic. Jesus, the kid is going to Europe! Mom would be over the moon, Timmy. You know she would."

Why couldn't he just say he was proud of me? Why did he have to summon up the specter of a woman I barely remembered?

"How's the deep freeze treating you?"

He hesitated. He didn't love talking about his work; the idea that one occupation defined a person never seemed to adhere to him.

"Just think warm, that's what I tell myself. Just think: Bermuda, Hawaii. Can't daydream too much though, all the activity flying around that warehouse. Actually," he said, changing gears, taking on a hopeful tone, "I've been hunting up new opportunities. They say things are really happening with this day-trading thing."

"Well, that's great, Dad. Good luck with that." I tried to sound like I meant it, and then, failing, tried a joke. "You always seem to have beginner's luck."

The life of a jazz musician: heroically stupid. The music was dead, embalmed, entombed; you could visit it now and then in the necropolis—the universities, the performing arts centers, Tuesday nights in subterranean coffees shops presided over by bald old dudes in kaftans and berets.

My father was among the last of the Boomers. He trusted in a world where a good man, a well-meaning man, could luck into a good, well-paying job. He still believed in being in the right place at the right time. But for me, a hundred, a thousand people were already lined up for the right time—though we all knew it had passed years ago. A little opportunity and a lot of education got us exactly nowhere. It seemed impossible that you might ever succeed. The Boomers got it all—the big cars, the big houses, the big gigs—and in their golden retirement (Jesus, if they ever bothered to retire), they'd still be pitying us for not living up to their youthful rebellion, for despising their middle-aged greed.

It's true that I was full of rage. My father never shared in the grand prosperity, and I blamed him for the meager circumstances in which I was beginning my own life. He was a man who never found any traction. When I was auditioning at North Texas, at Indiana, Berklee, and Oberlin, Dad was driving a delivery van for an old folks' home. When I was studying the sacred rhythms of the Yoruba and the jealously guarded chants and dances of Santería, he was busy speculating on domain names in the great stampede of the late nineties. He had a winner with beaniebabies.com, but softmicro.com and theunitedstatesofamerica.net never brought in the lucre. By the time I was old enough to make my pilgrimages to the Blue Note, the Vanguard, and Smalls Club, he was driving his Econoline around the Pacific Northwest, selling artisanal memorials and headstones — he argued that the catalog stuff was too impersonal. Just after I graduated North Texas, he started recruiting college kids to be exterminators. (I think he considered this his low point. He would go lower.) He traded the van for a VW custom-painted with a termite on the hood and the words "high-paying summer jobs!"

I came to Chicago just before the Towers fell in New York. Chicago was where the cutting-edge stuff, the truly *out* shit was happening, where they were mixing up free jazz with indie rock, Middle Eastern rhythms, chamber music, and whatever thumping chaos a computer could emit. New York felt like a closed shop, and I couldn't stomach the rent anyway. On the morning of the attacks, Dad called me, sick with fear. He needed reassurance: "You're not living near any tall buildings?" At the time, I was living out of my practice space in the West Loop but was loath to confess it to him. Dad was convinced the Sears Tower and Hancock Building were next. "Better get out of there for a few weeks, Tim. Come out here and stay with me."

I didn't bite. When the smoke cleared, he would realize the idea of my escaping to the rainy Northwest was ludicrous. And even if it wasn't, I also blamed him for leaving me without a home to go back to, for unmooring us both, for trying to start a new life for himself, and failing. Just before I went off to school, he sold the house I grew up in and followed a girlfriend (who left him soon enough) out there, seduced by the notion of sucking himself to the sleek and ravenous computer industry like a remora to a shark.

"You could get yourself set up in no time," he said that September morning. Hearing that he wouldn't even get a couple weeks out of me, he gallantly tried for more: a permanent reunion. "I hear they got a great music scene up in Seattle." He was a few years behind the times, but I didn't correct him. On the TV, the second tower was falling.

"I know, Dad," I said. "It's really happening out there."

"What's the latest from the bandstand?"
"Not much. SOS — same old shit."

For once, I didn't want to talk music. Charles Rigby had fucked me over. He'd hired a bunch of German cats as sidemen—cheaper for him—for the European tour. I wanted to lick my wounds, but I had to spend my Sunday teaching lessons, showing suburban brats how to bash along to Corrosion of Conformity and Godsmack. That night, I was playing with a country-rock band I was hoping to make pay. But this was a benefit show, meaning we worked free.

"What's the weather on your end?" I said.

"You get more sunny days than you'd think."

"Who needs a vacation, right?"

"Exactly." My father laughed, though I wouldn't have said it was funny. "You're right though. Most days it's gray as the afterlife out here. Still seeing that pretty girl you told me about?"

It had been a month and a half since I'd mentioned her, and I only said I was going on a date. Still, it was something for him to grab on to.

"I might see her tonight."

"A little romance maybe . . . ?" he said.

"Dad, enough already."

"All right, guy, all right. I'm hearing you. I get it—the life of a musician." On the other end, he no doubt winked knowingly. "Anyway, gotta go. Gotta catch a quick catnap. They put me on second shift. You know, it's not so bad once the blood gets moving. The team spirit kind of takes over."

"Well, stay warm," I said, the phrase that back home in the frozen north passed for both good will and good-bye.

I was teaching Brandan, my best student, a little thirteen-year-old grandee from Kenilworth, four-way independence and coordination. All that north-shore money had yet to refine his tastes. "This is jazz stuff," he said, throwing down his sticks in frustration. "What's the point of any of this?" I asked him if he'd heard Black Sabbath. "Yeah, bro," he said, "they're, like, *the* source for everything heavy."

"Well, all those cats came up on jazz: Django, Count Basie, Gene Krupa. Hell, the first Sabbath lineup had a guy playing tenor sax.

Here," I said, sitting down behind the kit and playing the first fill from "War Pigs." "That's Bill Ward. And this"—the intro to the first cut on *Caravan*—"is Art Blakey. What's the difference? The difference is Bill Ward tippy-tapped the drums, and Blakey *hit* them."

Brandan scowled, telling me this was all deeply uncool. But I knew that in a few months I'd put a Jazz Messengers record—*Free for All*, maybe—in this kid's hands, and it would blow him away.

On my way to the gig, my phone vibrated in my pocket—"Dad"—and I let it go to voice mail. I stopped by Azarello's for sticks. I walked into the drum department and there it was: a 1958 three-ply Gretsch Round Badge kit in Starlight Sparkle. I slipped into some kind of trance—I could see my future; this would be my instrument, my tubs, the sound that would define the rest of my performing life. "Old Drms + Cym $500," the price tag read. I picked up the cymbal, an original Turkish "K," recognizing it by the beautiful shimmer of its hammered surface. I glanced around jealously, thinking there must be ten other cats coming through the door going to beat me to it. There was only a guy sitting in guitars playing "Sweet Child of Mine" over and over. My cell phone buzzing again finally brought me back. Behind the counter, a skinny white dude was playing with the end of one his dreadlocks. I went up to him, pointed, and said, "I'll take it."

Then something told me to check my messages. It wasn't my father, but an unfamiliar, official-sounding voice explaining that my name was at the top of Dad's call history, saying there'd been an accident at the warehouse. Part of me was already calculating the cost of a flight to Oregon. Part of me was already mourning my lost Starlight Sparkle.

From the hospital window, I looked out and saw the seaside dunes and the mist that couldn't quite decide to be rain. I'd arrived just at the end of visiting hours, and they'd set me up on a cot in Dad's room. He'd grown his mustache back out—gray now, of course—along with a beard. I'd never seen him with one. His hair was shaggy, and it sat on his head strangely, like a wig.

"You look like you're in disguise, Dad," I said when the night nurse woke him to tell him I was there. "Getting ready to set out for the Arctic?"

He smiled distantly, like someone searching for a memory.

"What?" I said. "You thought I wouldn't come?"

They'd laid him out with some serious pain medication, and he was delirious. "Limeade," he said, wetting his lips to push the words out, "goddamn frozen limeade."

What happened, I learned, was that the shift manager at the loading bay had sent him deep into the high stacks of an arriving load to pluck out a forty-pound case of juice concentrate. Someone had stacked the pallet badly, and half the Minute Maid order toppled. A younger man with swifter reactions would've dodged; my father took it between his shoulders. Right place, right time.

I slept deeply next to him. Bless the silence of that hospital wing—I didn't get much silence in my life. But in the middle of the night I woke, aware of someone watching me. Dad sat on the edge of his bed in a gown that came to midthigh. His hands clutched the edge of the bed, his knuckles chapped and bruised—all that work in the freezer—like he'd just gone a few rounds.

"Beginner's luck, huh?" he said, looking so directly and intensely at me that I thought he must be seeing something else. "Tell me, what the fuck is that supposed to mean?"

"Pop," I said, having never called him "Pop" in my life. "You're high out of your mind."

"What's it mean?"

"Well, you got a lot of enthusiasm. You make friends easy. People like you, I guess."

"How do you live?" He strained forward like he was going to grab me, then suddenly sprang upright, seized by his spasming back, the cords of his neck popping out. "How do you live without any constants?" he said again when I'd settled him down.

"Any what?"

"I can't start from scratch again. I can't do it. What are we doing here? No time to waste. Come on, let's get out of this place."

He started up again, but I gently pushed him back down. "All right, Dad, lie down. Lie down now." I got him tucked in. "You want another shot? I can call them for another little shot of the good stuff."

"Mom's here," he said matter-of-factly. "Can't you feel her? She just came in a minute ago."

"I know, Dad, she's right here. Right here beside me."

I thought to get the night nurse, but then I just sat there sort of rubbing and petting his hand. Finally, I held his hand. I don't know how long. Long enough for the world to shrink to just that one room, the fog curling past the window one horizon, the dark hallway with its faint green glow the other. My mother. I suppose if she was anywhere that night, except under the ground, she was there with us, dancing somewhere between the vapor of my father's breath and my own, borne up again if only for a last few minutes.

In the morning, Dad was more himself again, flirting with the nurses, playacting the stoic but enfeebled old man giving himself into their tender care. They knew the routine but didn't seem to mind him. A doctor wearing Converse All Stars blew in and described some beautiful things: physical therapy, deep tissue massage, acupuncture. "You'll have discomfort from here on," he said, "so I want us all to think about ways we can manage your discomfort." Dad just grunted. I could already see the big tub of IcyHot coming out to live again on his bedside table. A pair of hairy knees slathered in mentholated ointment: the image of masculinity I carried all through childhood. When I was little, Dad liked to dab it on the tip of my nose. "Icy, then hot," he'd say, "icy, then hot," while I giggled uncontrollably.

When visiting hours started, his coworkers began filing in. Lots of joking around. Lots of "rest up now, old man." He had plenty of work buddies. Four months on the job, and he was already like a mascot to them. The shift manager showed around noon. "We hate seeing these kinds of accidents," he kept saying, "we just hate them." This man, I understood, was the company's messenger. You could smell the Freon coming off him. He asked Dad a hundred little questions: How's the food? You got enough pillows? What do you think you'll do? Why don't you take a few weeks? Take your time, rest up, don't go pushing yourself too hard.

Dad turned to me, a helpless look on his face. "Have you met my son?" he said. "He's one of the best jazz drummers in the country."

"Come on now, Dad," I protested in my modesty.

"You like jazz?" Dad asked his boss.

"Sure, yeah," the shift manager said uneasily, "all that jazz."

My phone vibrated in my pocket. The display listed a long, strangely formatted number: Europe. I hesitated. "Oops," I said on the fourth ring, "gotta take this." I went out in the hall. It was Charles Rigby telling me that Ernst, the Bavarian drummer he'd hired to replace me, couldn't swing for shit. "Mr. Tim," Charles said in that legendary raspy voice, "get your white ass over here."

"All right, Charles," I said, "sounds good, sounds good. Listen, I'll talk to you soon." I snapped the phone shut on him midsentence.

"They've been in meetings all morning," the shift manager was telling Dad when I came back in. "They're taking this thing seriously. I mean, you've really got them on the ropes." Dad hardly seemed to be listening. He was staring out the window, at what little he could see of the dunes. "You'll have discomfort sure, but this is the kind of thing—well, you'll never have to work another day in your life."

Dad set his jaw, trying to harden himself. But I was there to see, the instant it began, the waste setting in. Over the two years he had left, he must have started twenty or thirty different armchair hobbies. Seagram's Whiskey and Winston cigarettes were two of them, but they were not the things that killed him.

The nurses came in and kicked both me and the shift manager out so they could change the sheets and get Dad cleaned up. "I'll be right back, Pop," I called out. "I'm going to pick up some of your stuff." In the hallway, the shift manager shook my hand. "I'll look out for your name," he told me.

I got directions to Dad's apartment on the outskirts of town. I was charged with picking up a change of clothes, some books and magazines, and a few other things to keep him distracted. As I drove through the misty streets of Florence, I couldn't help it—I did the math: if I got a flight out of PDX by early evening, I'd make it in time to meet Charles at the Düsseldorf Jazz Rally. It wouldn't even be a question of asking Dad's forgiveness. He of all people would understand.

The apartment was tidy and small, exceptionally small. Dad had built shelves on almost every wall, and his rooms were filled with the fresh, astringent scent of bare pine. I went into the bedroom and picked out a couple plaid shirts. There weren't more than a few to choose from; he didn't have anything other than work clothes. In the dresser, his underwear was ironed and perfectly folded—the man had time on his hands. I threw together an overnight bag as quickly as I could. I was rushing now; it was going to be a matter of minutes, not hours.

I dropped the bag at the door and used the toilet. But then, hurrying out, I stopped in my tracks. Between a small library of sci-fi paperbacks, framed by them as it were, were photos, certificates, ribbons, a little trophy of a tiny man wailing away on saxophone. "Outstanding Soloist," the attached plaque read.

He'd built a shrine to me, like he'd built one to my dead mother in the house I grew up in: a photo of me sitting at a club, up close to the stage, watching Elvin Jones play, leaning over intently, studying his every move. Another of me unpacking my first drum set. A dumb teenage drawing of a concert, flames shooting up from the stage, and all the spotlights turned on me.

What can be said about it? There was no time to linger. I felt embarrassed and shy to see that here, in this obscure corner of nowhere, I'd already made it.

Lost
Coast

He wasn't difficult to find. For a time, in the small little world I inhabit, he was everywhere. These days all you need is six songs and some blog traffic to make people believe you might be a homespun genius, a blessed saint, a prophet of the unconscious. I got his number from his record label—press connections—and called him up.

"Well, fuck me, Walt." His midwestern twang was mixed up now with a California drawl. "It's pretty fantastic to hear from you. I mean, shit, I was just thinking about you the other day. How the hell you doing? You doing good?"

"Not as good as you. You're blowing up out there, aren't you?"

"Aw, man, just a run of luck."

I went on about how great the EP sounded, practiced in my art of inflated praise. He begged off, talked about his collaborators and how the spirit of the old lighthouse they'd recorded vocals in had infused the tracks with something somehow ancient, a kind of lonely vigilance.

"Shit, come on out!" he said when I mentioned I might be heading out west for a few days. To check out the SF scene, I said, maybe write about it for the Web site. "Stay with me and my girl. We'd love to have you. Man, it's been too long. I can't believe it, you and me, making it in the same business! This is cool. This feels really right to me."

I knew that he was just about to start recording his first full-length album. I said I didn't want to disturb him during the creative process.

"The first full-length anyone will actually *hear*," he said, laughing at his own expense. Meaning all the rest had been ignored, but now that he was trading on his past, his story, he was finally getting some attention. "Nah, Walt, you gotta come stay with me and Vanessa. I've told her so much about you."

Meaning, he'd told her about John.

"I'll check into a hotel. Don't want to put you and your girl out."

But, then, just at the last minute, just as I was getting on my flight at O'Hare, I called him again, asked if I could crash after all. I hadn't even booked a room, but I lied and said my reservation had gotten lost in the system. Keaton faltered for a moment, then said, "Sure, man, crash with us."

That's when I knew it would all go my way.

———

Keaton Wilding, the *County B Submarine* EP. On the flight, I listened on repeat, ten times or more. Stereogum: "An astonishing debut. Wilding's tormented past gives staggering depth to songs that, on first listen, seem like simply more blissed-out California pop." Popmatters: "Wilding assembles a ramshackle cast of San Francisco musicians to craft a sound that seduces and sucker-punches. If Brian Wilson and Syd Barrett had a love child, he would be named Keaton." All the most fickle Web sites and magazines, the "tastemakers," were falling over each other to herald his arrival. Only the Web site I wrote for, on which all the reviewers are anonymous, had tried to stem the tide: "Capable, but shallow. The kind of bleary-eyed confession that wears itself out quick."

We were from the same small town. Keaton was two grades behind me. I'd known him through John; the two of them, along with their friend Mason, were hardly apart. I remembered Keaton playing Snowdaze, our winter talent show. Dressed in Birkenstocks and a ball cap, cradling a Taylor acoustic, he sat at the front of the school cafeteria and covered some god-awful song by Phish or String Cheese Incident or August Rawling Band, one of those jam bands still carrying the sputtering torch of the Dead. Keaton and John were always driving off to Alpine Valley or the World to see those late-night spectacles: thirty thousand people, each in their own private dream, twirling and weaving to twenty-minute guitar solos. It was the drugs, not the music, that snared John. And the drugs came from Keaton.

Keaton hit the last chord of the song; the cafeteria echoed with applause. At the senior table, my friends and I smirked—that bullshit stoner music was laughable to us. Back then I was way ahead of the game. All I listened to was free jazz, Bulgarian women's choirs, Charles Ives, and the Residents (the early albums).

Keaton and his girl lived in an apartment way out by the beach. "We've got the best view in town," Keaton said as he led me out the bedroom window and up a narrow ladder to the roof. He lit a Parliament, leaned on the railing, and stared out in the direction of the sea. You could only hear the waves. It was too foggy to see anything other than the tops of a few frumpy sand dunes.

"Vanessa apologizes. She's over in Oakland with the guys from Silent Partner. She's doing some woodcuts for their album art and a few show posters. You should review them. Their new record is gonna be rad."

"I heard their last one, *Deadly Silent*. Reminded me of Secret Machines." Not intended as praise.

"They're such sweet guys too," Keaton went on. "They've really helped me out along the way. We've played a bunch of shows together." He ground out his cigarette on the railing and turned to me, and for a brief moment we met eyes and I saw in his a question — *What are you doing here?*

We went back inside. He got us a couple beers and flopped down on the couch. The sandals and ball cap were gone, replaced by threadbare cords, a faded Members Only jacket, and, the latest in affectations, a pair of boat shoes, no socks. Clothes chosen as a parody of clothes. He still wore his hair long, but sheathed now in a week's worth of grease. The Taylor was gone from sight; in the living room, the beat-up Fender Jazzmaster pictured on the cover of the EP hung from a peg. The burden he carried was more proudly displayed. It was there in every gesture, the way he narrowed his eyes when he took a drag, sighed when he cracked a beer. No more Keystone Light, the swill he, Mason, and John used to drink driving around in Mason's Jeep. Out here it was Tecate with a wedge of lime.

"How's it going with the Web site?" he asked me. "You digging it?"

"It sure doesn't pay the bills."

"You probably get a ton of free music though."

"Everyone gets free music these days," I said.

"Don't I know it. That kind of shit doesn't bug you until you get a record deal. I quit my day job," he confessed, seeming embarrassed about it. "It's cool, we're more or less getting by. But it kind of puts the pressure on. To, you know, 'succeed.'"

"The EP is doing great."

"Yeah." He laughed. "Man, we didn't have a fucking clue what we were doing with that one. I mean —" He hesitated, suddenly unsure of himself in a way that made him almost unrecognizable to me — "I was so fucking fried the whole time. What the hell were we thinking — recording in a *lighthouse*?" He sighed, popped another Tecate. "So, we're booked for this session at Hyde Street Studios on Friday. Want to come with?"

Come with. He still had a little of the Midwest in him.

"I wouldn't want to get in your way."

"Nope. Come on down. It'd be cool to have you there."

Maybe he thought I'd write about it for the Web site, get a little early buzz going. Maybe he wanted me there as a reminder of John.

"I'd be honored," I said.

We drank beer and listened to records. For all the specialized knowledge we had in common, we ran out of conversation quick, now that business had been taken care of. I said I was getting sleepy. Jet lag. He made up the couch for me. Just before he turned in, he made himself some peppermint tea. He said it helped keep his vocal cords loose.

I descend the staircase. Stand out in the street, trembling. A finger of fog drifts toward me, passes through my body. Am I alive? These things that haunt me . . . the Jeep "submarines" under the truck trailer. We speak, it seems so real. *Didn't I tell you? Don't go with them.* More real than this life. A foghorn sounds, very far away. Then I feel him, I feel him. He's there, at the corner, waiting where the murk meets darker night. I quicken my pace. He grows more distant, a patch of dark gray against the dark. Headlights brush past me, a wall of air; I brace for the collision. *Don't go. Don't go.* And then the lights come on.

I sat up on the couch. "Oh, sorry to wake you." Keaton's girl. "You're Walt, right?" She hung her coat on the doorknob, swept her hair over her shoulders. I let the jealousy play back and forth inside me. Beautiful, of course she was beautiful.

"It's me," I said, still half in that other world.

"You freaked me out there for a second. Sorry, K said you were staying."

She made tea. This time I accepted. She was tired but jumpy. Yes, I had frightened her. I could see it in those bright, startled eyes.

"Is it snowing in Chicago?"

"It's been too fucking cold to snow in Chicago." She flinched at my hard words, then pretended she hadn't. She blinked, yawned.

"I'm here covering the SF scene," I said, mock-serious. "Tell me, what's it like having a rock-star boyfriend?"

"I've seen him play too many half-empty clubs. I've seen him play too many *empty* clubs. So I don't mind him getting some exposure. Anyway, if he ever writes a song called 'Vanessa,' I'm out of here." She didn't wear sarcasm well. She was too young, too translucent for it. "What's it like being a critic?"

"You know what they say: Too dumb to be an intellectual, too ugly to be a rocker." Why this tone, this constant sneer? I must draw it out in people. I told the last woman I dated that I was starting to fall in love her. And she laughed, said, Sure you are. "I've got a straight job as well," I said. "I work in an office."

"Me too." Vanessa poured the tea. "Keaton says it was your younger brother who was in the accident. It must be strange for you, knowing it could just have easily been Keaton who died."

"It's not strange. I think about it every day."

"I'm sorry. You must miss your brother."

I didn't answer, played the stoic act, refusing to let anyone else limit my suffering. But her eyes held me there, suspended in my anger, which suddenly felt weightless, futile.

"He's glad you're here," she said. "He couldn't stop talking about it when you called. It feels right to him that you're here."

"That's what he told me."

"He means it. He keeps in pretty close touch with his feelings."

"California must do that to everyone."

"Yeah," she said, "I guess it does."

In the morning, I was up before either of them. I eased open their door, watched them sleeping. Keaton had his arm tight around her. He held on to her like a man about to drown.

———

That afternoon, he and I walked the length of Golden Gate Park. He told me about the album, about the preproduction work he'd been doing, tweaking each song and each part. The EP had been self-recorded, self-produced, self-released—a miracle it'd ever gotten finished. Whatever drug came his way, he'd crawled inside it, curled up, and tried to live in that brief moment of emptiness, vision, and paralysis. Making the EP had nearly killed him, but what was worse was that its success felt arbitrary: There were thousands of twenty-five-year-old dudes out there writing songs just as good, singing them with all the conviction and desperation he'd known since he'd left the Midwest and begun his wanderings. The EP had been a heartfelt mess; he wanted the full-length to be polished, the harmonies tight, the arrangements crafty and unexpected, the playing assured but not wanky. He was clean now and moving into his late twenties, with Vanessa at his side, with a record deal, a career to make for himself. They were rerecording "County B Submarine," and it would be the centerpiece of the record. He needed to prove that he wasn't just some lo-fi fluke.

Maybe he thought he was being interviewed, or he was just trying to fill up the silence I let hang between us. The album he described was the very definition of a sophomore flop. We walked all the way to Hippie Hill, at which point Keaton asked if we could turn back. He tried to stay clear of the Haight—too much temptation. At one point he actually told me he was trying to "save himself" through music.

We walked for a long time without speaking. It was getting toward evening, and the fog was slipping in again. Off in the distance I saw a herd of buffalo. The sails of a windmill turned above wind-stunted trees. We walked further into the murk.

"After the accident," Keaton began, "I thought I could keep it together. My folks sent me to all these counselors, but I figured I was fine. I went up to the UW, thought maybe I'd study music theory, get a degree." He shook his head, amazed at the innocence of those notions. I already knew what he told me next, the wayward history that all the toadying bloggers had been so ravenous to relate: After a year or so of college, going through the motions, Keaton had disappeared. He'd sold all his possessions, his clothes, his Taylor guitar. He'd hitched. He'd even tried to ride the rails. In Kansas and Texas, and especially on one rabid night in Montezuma, New Mexico, for which he had a jagged pink scar across his belly as a reminder, he'd had to claw his way out of some seriously stupid follies. For a time, he wandered up and down the West Coast, astonished by the living, crumbling grandeur of it, finally finding a home of sorts on the black sand beaches of Humboldt County. He lived there in anonymity among the wasters and the growers, sheltering in an improvised hut, spending his days and nights observing the seabirds and the constantly shifting map of the endless dark waves. Then, on his twentieth birthday, or what he estimated to be his twentieth birthday, he reemerged in San Francisco and began to write songs and gather a group of musicians around him.

There was something mechanical about this monologue, as if he'd been rehearsing it since we'd first spoken on the phone. What was I there to say? What did he want me to say? He told me about the junk, the pilfered prescription meds, the nightmare days and nights spent faltering through an approximation of a musician's life. He certainly had the gift for self-dramatization. After John died, I hadn't even known how to burn out, only to do what my father had: drink myself toward a leaden sleep every night of the week. I'd quietly kept it up till about a year ago, when my weak stomach finally said enough. My story paled in comparison, and besides, I wanted him to talk, to exhaust these things he'd learned by heart. Finally, he reached a moment's quiet.

"That night," I said. "Whose idea was it?"

He looked at me, wild-eyed.

"Whose idea was it to what?"

"To get all piss drunk and stoned and drive two hours to a concert."

"That's what we did pretty much every weekend."

"Who bought the beer?"

"I don't remember," he said. Then he admitted, "Probably I did. I had the best fake."

"I know that Mason was driving. Why'd you let him drive drunk?"

"He always did. I don't know, we never really thought about it."

"Then what happened, after the beer?"

There wasn't much to tell, but I made him give me all the details. They slammed a couple Keystones each on the way out of town; Keaton handed John his sack and John started rolling a joint. The stereo blasted Phish, or maybe it was Darkstar. (Jesus, to have that be the last music to hear in life . . .) They bullshitted about a chick

John had been boning, killed a few more beers, talked about what they'd do that summer, the summer after they all graduated, last summer of freedom.

As Keaton went on, as the Jeep slipped through the night, I felt all that distance covered. The life Keaton described was just the simple, stupid life of teenagers, and yet I abhorred it. I felt John pulling away from me all over again, from the way I'd tried to show him (which was really just the way of our honest, self-effacing, workaholic father). Keaton and John—they were insep-arable. But it hadn't been so long ago that John and I were riding bikes together, playing war out in the woods, crawling into the same sleeping bag under a tiny cabin made of couch cushions and a bed sheet draped over the backs of chairs. When we got too old and too self-conscious for roughhousing and making forts, we shared music; I felt so proud when John went out and spent his paper route money on some overpriced, atrociously recorded Pavement or Uncle Tupelo bootleg, just to win my approval. We'd listen to those hissy live documents all night, trying to feel what it was like, to be there at the concert, to feel the music moving something inside us. Then Keaton came along, and with him came partying and girls, and John grew up so quick I hardly had time to see that he'd already been taken from me.

"Viscera"—I woke up at the word, and Keaton was describing how he woke up too, and there was a sweet, wet smell all around him and the cold wind blowing through where the front of the Jeep had been. He looked down at his hands; they were working, as if by reflex, picking the viscera of his two friends off his new pair of jeans. (He didn't say "guts" or "blood." Maybe he was trying to spare me.) He forced open the rear, passenger-side door, stumbled out into the night. A voice called to him, the driver of the eighteen-wheeler—"Hey, kid!"—but Keaton just kept going, and it wasn't till he felt the truck driver's hand on his shoulder that he understood what had happened.

I could hear the waves now. Across the Great Highway, there was nothing but the ragged sand dunes, the fog hanging above the sea, a few small fires burning on the beach.

"How'd you survive?" Keaton said. "After John died."

"You know that Neutral Milk Hotel song 'Two-Headed Boy'? I used to put that on and just weep."

Now I couldn't even listen to it.

"I love that song," Keaton said reverently. "Major inspiration." We crossed the highway and walked along the dunes. "Listen, I'm glad we had this talk." He put his hand on my shoulder, a hand reaching across the years. Perhaps he believed things were settled between us now. He told me he had to get to band practice. There was still plenty to be done before the session. "Do you know your way back home? Van will be there."

"Sure, I'm good. I'm cool."

But when we parted ways, I turned and went the opposite direction, needing to be alone and to despise everything in sight. I wandered through the park all the way to Haight and Ashbury: gutter punks, half-starved dogs, the whole grim pageant of begging and peddling. A guy stopped me on the street. "Hey, brother, what do you need?"

"I need a lot of things," I said. "The question is what do you have?"

***

Vanessa was working at the kitchen table. We listened to the new Black Moth Super Rainbow. I went over and watched over her shoulder, breathed her in, the faint sharp smell of sweat—she hadn't washed since last night—her own sex, Keaton's. The wood curled up under her grooved knife. She blew across the block to clear the shavings. It was taking shape—an intricate, towering coastline, a lone car traveling a winding road, the surf booming down below, her knife catching both the subtle spray and the monolithic cliffs. "Just an idea for K's new album," she said. I could tell I was fussing her concentration, but I stayed there watching, imagining my fingers running through her hair.

"I like how the cliffs are out of proportion with the rocks. Very German."

"He's nervous," she said. "He's been working the guys too hard. They'll go way late tonight."

"You're a band widow. It happens."

The conversation went from there, her catalog of Keaton's failings, my sympathetic murmurs. We moved to the bedroom. . . .

She held her knife up to the light. "I've dated musicians before," she said. "They're a fun time. But Keaton's only gotten more serious since I've known him. It scared me at first." She blew a sliver of wood from the knife's groove, and I trembled. "But he's going after something. Doesn't it make your job hard, telling everyone how far they fall short?"

I slipped her shirt from her shoulders. She pushed Keaton's clothes off the bed, took me in her arms. . . .

"Sometimes the best stuff is just an accident."

"If you want something good to happen, you put yourself in a good place."

"Artistic maturity," I said. "That's a dangerous step."

"Well," she said, looking at me for the first time, "what other choice is there?"

The car took on headlights, they coned out into the darkness. The sea got stormy. The waves grew taller. She said she was hungry. I said I was hungry too. Do you want a peanut butter sandwich? Sure. We sat eating in silence. After a time, she said she was going to check in on Keaton, went into the bedroom to call him, and closed the door.

That night, alone on the couch, I reached for myself, and undressed her again.

The session started at four the next afternoon and was set to run till four that night. Keaton and I got off the streetcar downtown and walked among the shambling deco buildings. On one corner, a torn rag of a woman wearing a leg brace was out cold facedown. We passed a homeless guy selling old clothes and VHS tapes, his wares spread out on a blanket. "Check it out," Keaton said, picking up a red plastic telescope, a child's toy, and handing it to me. I could just make out a large, blurry image—a naked woman spread-eagled—a photo cut out and pasted to the lens. "Someone different is selling this every week," Keaton said. "Never fails." We stopped at a rundown building, went through an unmarked door and up several flights of stairs. Gleaming hardwood floors, banks of electronics steadily blinking, a huge console with sliders and knobs, like something NASA used before computers shrank—the studio itself was immaculate. In the control room, the engineer was sunk in the broken-down middle of a ratty couch, eating a bucket of KFC, a microphone he'd been fiddling with cradled in his lap.

"What up, Brodie?" Keaton said, doing a complicated handshake with the engineer. "Ready to get this shit started?" He introduced me as a friend from back home.

"This is the A room," Keaton said, showing me around with obvious pride. "Neve board, two-inch tape, plate reverb, Neumann mics . . . They don't use this stuff much anymore. No one can afford it." He reached down and twisted a knob on the console, lost for a moment in its beautiful complexity. Then, regaining his modesty: "The record company gave us a little chunk of change, but it's still only good for, like, a day in here."

Fifteen minutes later, the band started to file in, carrying guitars and drums, an accordion, a celesta, a glockenspiel, a zanzithophone. "All right, boys, this is Walt, an old buddy from back in Wisco."

Bass: "What's poppin, Holmes?"

Lead guitar: "Cool to meet you."

Drums: "Whoa, firm handshake. Hey, man, I need that hand to play with."

Bass: "To beat off with, you mean."

Keys, winds, accordion, glock, keytar, everything else: "Yeah, same fucking difference. Wisco, Wisco, Wisco. How is it *hangin*, Walter? Mr. Music Critic. Better write some good shit about this shit."

They were your typical bunch of wasters—longhaired, glassy-eyed disciples of their instruments who could break your heart with a string bend, a rim click, a doubled lead—who in ten years would probably be redoing the siding on your house. Seeing the way they shrugged their way into the live room to begin setting up and tuning, I felt the urgency again, that burning feeling trying to get out of me. How long had I wanted to explain to people? There were no ideas in music, only touch and instinct and sometimes grace—the mechanical virtues—and that among those who were given the tools, only a few, a scant few, would be able to tell you something true. I had tried to teach John these things, how to dismiss all the false prophets. In the control room, Keaton was drinking his peppermint tea. He tipped his head back and massaged his throat. He looked like a baby bird feeding.

The engineer went into the live room and started positioning mics. Keaton dogged his every move. "I want this to sound *live*," he kept saying. "I want tons of bleed and, like, zero overdubs. I want to hear the *room*, you know? The *wood*."

Finally, everything was set up. The band gathered in a loose circle, Keaton in the middle with his Jazzmaster slung over his shoulder. The engineer leaned back in his chair and set the tape machine rolling. "All right, fellas," he said through the talkback mic, "how about a little first-take magic?"

"Let's run the hot-chick song," Keaton said to his band. He'd told me he never named his songs until they were recorded. " . . . two, three, four!" The drummer flubbed the very first entrance. Everyone in the live room laughed. Nerves. They couldn't afford many mistakes like that. Keaton counted it off again.

The song was about a hot chick Keaton had seen once at Rickshaw Stop. The lyrics were throwaway, an expression of sexual longing and potency that fell away in the last verse to affirm his reignited faithfulness to his girl. The song had B side stamped all over it; hearing it, you wondered why you wasted your own words trying to describe this libidinal chaff. And then the slide guitar took the melody and ascended into the chorus, the bass pedaled on its E string, the drums dropped into a loose, half-time shuffle, Keaton's voice wavered on the last note of "No, babe, no, I ain't looking ba-*aaaa*-ck," and all your objections quietly slipped away.

The engineer turned to me. "Pain in my ass, but he sure can write a hook."

They ran the song a few more times, then came in for the playback. "Hell, yes!" Keaton said, bouncing on the balls of his feet. "Listen to that motherfuckin' *reverb*! Phil Spector would cream his pants if he heard that shit." Keaton danced around the room, only pausing to make himself more tea.

"I'll get it for you," I told him.

The next two songs came easy—a countrified romp with MIDI sax solo, then a slice of fuzzed-out psychedelia about making love in the Marin County headlands—the playing loose and confident, the groove huge, wooly, and barking on the low end. How far a band can come in a year! Everything hits harder; there's no searching, just this vast canyon of sound that suddenly opens up before you. And Keaton's voice . . . On the EP it had been reedy, slightly metallic-sounding, hemmed in by the conical confines of the lighthouse. These vintage tube mics opened things up: the way he threw himself past the boundaries of his range, the ragged falsetto that leapt heedlessly over the volume thrown up by the band, the throaty little yelp with which he ended every phrase. He'd fry his voice in ten years if he kept up like this, but right now he was dashing ahead, lost in the thrill of being pursued, stumbling joyously, scoffing at what quarried him, knowing that with every step he was gaining, gaining.

Keaton called "County B Submarine." He looked through the glass at me, nodded. So, he did want me here. He was using me, not for exposure but to bring that hopeless loss and terror home again.

The song began with a tricky acoustic line that got even trickier as the electric started to wind around it. This was the sort of thing easily solved with overdubs, but Keaton insisted on the purity of live takes and the parts bleeding together on tape. Oh, yes, he was old school, all the way. The engineer switched on the talkback. "Want to try that again?"

"It's D# on the second change," Keaton told his guitarist.

"Nah, man, it's D."

Keaton played through it by himself. "Yeah, you're right. What the fuck? I've played this a thousand times." That probably wasn't an exaggeration.

"They start off okay," the engineer said to me, "then get self-conscious. They'll settle down after a while."

After a couple more takes, they got through the intro. The band snuck in, vamping on a claustrophobic diminished chord. Night started to gather. The road wound ahead, funneling you into the inevitability of the verse. All possibilities narrowed down to one. Keaton's voice climbed high, perched on a height, teetered. He sang about old grain silos and shuddering fields of grain, about a vast great lake shimmering, white geese landing on its mirrored surface. As they played, Keaton stared at me. He was singing about our home. And though I'd heard all these lyrics before, I understood now how far he'd traveled. For him, that home was the afterlife, where he could never go, and his friends were still traveling along one endless road, searching for the border and never reaching it. "And if you go over," Keaton sang, and I had to swallow a hard knot in my throat, "I'll go over too."

Then, in the middle of the bridge, he stopped, waved his hands. Stop, stop, stop.

"What's up?" the engineer said.

"Doesn't feel right," Keaton muttered. He turned to the keyboardist. "What about arpeggiating that sus chord? And maybe play it on the Rhodes, not the Hammond?"

The keyboardist shrugged. "I guess."

They shuffled things around, played the song again. But the take sounded limp, lusterless. Keaton made more changes. At one point, he sat down behind the drum kit and showed the drummer what to play. They ran the song again. It fell apart in the first chorus. "Fuck," Keaton said. "I just hear it different in here, you know?" He tapped the side of his skull. "This room is fucking with me." He pressed ahead. He didn't want to waste any time; he was paying nine hundred bucks an hour to use this legendary studio. They ran the song again. Another train wreck.

"All right," Keaton said, shaking his head, "let's take a break, chill out, drink a couple beers."

"I was just about to say that," the engineer said over the talkback.

The band straggled into the control room. They listened to the playback on "County B Submarine." I could see their ears perk up. The second take was *it*—until Keaton stopped in the bridge. "Maybe we could dump it into Pro Tools, splice together a vocal?" the engineer said.

"No digital," Keaton insisted. "We can get this in one take."

"Let's just play it like we always do," the bassist said.

The rest of the band agreed. They were tired now, disheartened. It was past midnight. They'd been playing for six straight hours.

"Yeah," Keaton said, sipping his tea, a clouded look on his face, "yeah, let's do it like always."

I'd been watching all of this in silence, but now I pushed myself off the couch, reached into my pocket. "Fellas," I said pulling out a Ziploc bag and unrolling it. "Maybe these will help." The mushrooms were gnarled and desiccated, a sickly gray-yellow, almost pulsating with poison. They gathered round.

"Holy shit," the bass player said, his jaw hanging open.

"Oh, man, I shouldn't play fucked-up."

"What are you talking about, bro? You're stoned right now."

"Shit, those are some serious-looking spores. You know, scientists say Psilocybin came here from space, on a fucking meteor. There's a giant mushroom floating in the center of the galaxy, like a giant brain, and it's communicating with us through the shrooms."

"Man, you've been reading those Web sites again."

"They're mellow," I said, glancing over at Keaton. "Come on, you guys sound tight. You need something to get that feeling, that spontaneity."

He looked on, wavering. It had worked before. He'd made the EP under the influence. I could almost tell myself I was trying to help him, that his longing for purity would be his undoing, that no one wanted to hear a perfect album anyway — why not indulge in amateurism again? The moment arrived when he should have told his band no, and then it passed.

"Fuck it," the bass player said, reaching in and grabbing a couple stems and a couple caps. "We need to loosen up some."

They divided the bag in four. "K, you want some?" Keaton couldn't look at me. I couldn't look at him. But it didn't matter what he did now. The decision had been made for him already.

I'd been spiking his tea for hours.

The band went back into the live room and began to fuck around on their instruments. They tried to run "County B" a few more times. "I dig what you were saying before," the guitarist said to Keaton, "but why don't we change it to this?" He played a long, spiraling lead part, much longer than the bridge itself, then trailed off into directionless noodling. The switch had flipped. The drummer was lost in the plaid cushions of the live-room couch. He sat on his stool, playing lazily, but his gaze was locked on those cushions. The keyboardist held one chord, leaned over his Hammond organ, listening. With his free hand, he kept flipping switches, changing the sound by tiny degrees. "This chord is, like, mystic," I heard him murmur over his mic. "Fucking Scriabin, man."

"Simplify," the drummer said, "just simplify."

Keaton counted off the song. Collectively, they went for a more primitive approach, the drummer thudding away on his floor tom, the bassist popping and slapping all up and down the fretboard, the keyboardist flipping switches and twiddling knobs, emitting swooping, sirenlike noises. Keaton tried to concentrate. He bore down and tried to get through. But it came apart. Losing first a wheel, then an axle, and then collapsing into a rolling, tumbling mess, it came completely apart.

"Don't leave me," he said. "Just don't leave me." I'd gotten him into a cab, taken him back out to the ocean. We'd passed up the apartment and come down to the beach. Whatever fires had been burning that night had long gone out. I slung his arm over my shoulder, and we stumbled down to where the fog met the waves. Everything was moving, and at the same time, it was still, as if here at the edge of the world, it all dissolved into contradictions. "I can get more money," he said. "They believe in me." The record label, his fans, Vanessa, his band—yes, they all believed in him. He'd made a life for himself out here from almost nothing. "I can get more studio time."

He was right. He'd be in and out of that studio, and several others, for nearly two years. *Lost Coast* would be released to critical acclaim and, thanks to an instrumental track featured in an iPod ad, moderately strong sales. Keaton was on his way to becoming a songwriter's songwriter, known for his relentless excavation of his past, his meticulousness, and the way he churned through backing musicians. He toured constantly, and his onstage behavior grew erratic, his rambling, pseudoprophetic between-song banter becoming part of his appeal for the coterie. Finally, Vanessa left him and took her woodcuts to New York, where she collaborated with and eventually married a noted graphic novelist. Of course, for Keaton, there was always another girl waiting in the next town. They practically lined up to save him.

He turned to me. His pupils were the size of dimes. "I can get more studio time, you know that, right?" When I didn't reply, he said, "I don't blame you, Walt. I don't blame you for hating me."

I threw him down on the wet sand. I wouldn't let him say it, that of all things—I wouldn't let him say he forgave me. He might get everything else, but the one thing I would take from him was redemption, even if it was my own.

A wave rushed up and knocked us both over. The water fizzled around us as it receded. As we rose, Keaton pointed down the beach, about half a mile away—"There!" A last fire burning, a dark figure moving at its edges, slipping in and out of the light. It was John. For an instant, he was there.

"Don't you see?" Keaton said. "Don't you *see?*"

But already the fire was gone, swallowed by the dark and the waves. I dragged us toward it, but I knew it was gone. After that night, John would never again visit me unbidden—only when I put on that goddamn record and pushed play.

Coda

I was taller and also stronger than Luke, so I went first through the window into Kate's kitchen. I'd done it a couple of other times, when Kate and I had gotten ourselves locked out. Outside, Luke's boots frantically scraped the brick wall. He called out—"Tim, Tim, come on, help me, man," and I thought, If this doesn't bring the cops . . .

I stuck my head out the window. Luke was clutching the sill, his fingers white, his eyes practically popping out of his skull. I grabbed both his wrists and pulled. He was so skinny he came through all at once, and I fell back and landed hard enough on my butt to rattle a cat dish sitting at the base of the sink. I listened for voices, the neighbors coming to the door to see what the hell was going on. We were lucky the building was full of Lincoln Park singles sleeping heavily after another night of barhopping. Luke stood looking down at me, his teeth gleaming faintly in the dark. He was smiling. "Yes, sir, we are in," he said. "Hard part's over."

He crossed the room and started sliding his hand along the wall, searching for the light switch. "Let me," I said. I found the switch, no problem. Six months hadn't killed the muscle memory. Luke and I stood there blinking against the light. The kitchen stretched out around us—black marble, brushed aluminum, bamboo flooring.

"Sweet digs, right?" Luke said. "Shit, the good life." Sweat stood out on his forehead, and his red hair was in matted disarray. He looked like a kid who'd just come in from playing in the snow instead of a grown man shambling into his thirties. He pulled a black ski mask from his pocket and drew it down crookedly over his face. "*Hey*," he said, "put your mask on."

"What's the point?" I went over and closed the window. "We're already inside."

I went into the living room and found the light there, then into the small room I used to have as my music studio. Kate had converted it into a home office. A chaos of paperwork from her law practice was spread across the desk. She'd brought in her stuff from storage, and boxes were stacked everywhere. There were gallon cans of wall paint and painting supplies, but in the months she'd been living in the apartment alone she'd painted only one wall. Baby blue. That was as far as her fresh start had gone.

In the living room, nearly all our old furniture was gone. Some I'd taken with me; the rest she'd replaced with Crate and Barrel stuff. Where I used to have a big framed poster of Clifford Brown and Art Blakey playing Birdland, she'd hung black and whites of her family: her dead mom, her booze-hound dad, her two eternally bickering brothers. Kate was down in Key West now on an emergency visit to her middle brother, Eldridge. Over the last year he'd set off on a one-man mission to snort up all the coke on the islands.

Luke came in. "This takes balls," he announced. He'd straightened his mask, and I watched his chapped lips moving inside the mouth slit. "What we're doing tonight takes seriously big nuts."

At least I wouldn't have to look at his face while we searched the apartment. "Not bad for a couple regular cats. I mean, shit, this is like a victory for guys everywhere."

"Fine. Good. Let's get to it already."

"We got all night, Tim. We got time to explore." He drew out that last word in a way that made my skin prickle.

Three weeks back, Luke had shown up at the Green Mill. I was playing with my trio. He came in around midnight, squeezed into a booth up front. I figured he was there waiting to sit in on the late night jam, hanging around like he always did, but he didn't even have his horn. After our last set, he came up to me with two doubles of Maker's. *Heard something about you and Kate,* he said. *Heard she never gave your ring back. Guess what, man? She never gave mine back either.*

I nodded toward a stack of boxes. "I'll work on these. You start in the bedroom." It was the one room I didn't want to invade.

Luke's eyes narrowed, dialed in like he was spotting me from a distance. My skin prickled again. The one thing Kate had liked about him was that he was intense. That's what Kate's friend Holly told me anyway.

"Take *all* the jewelry," I said. "We need to make this look real."

The idea was we'd create a little mess and, in addition to what we came for, swipe a few small, impersonal things Kate could get replaced on insurance. We'd make it look like the kind of quick score the junkies who congregated underneath the L stop were always hankering to pull off. The cops wouldn't even take a second look. And if Kate suspected anyone, I figured she'd suspect Luke.

He clapped his hands—"Let's do this thing"—and strolled into the bedroom.

I started picking through a box. Empty CD cases, old bills, boxes of checks, and, wrapped up in newspaper, novelty martini glasses in the shape of palm trees. Kate was a precise, organized woman, but she never could throw anything away. The next box was instruction manuals, postcards, hair clips. Getting the rings back might not be the easy job Luke and I had drunkenly envisioned. "We need our rings back," Luke said that night at the Mill. "We *deserve* them back."

Two months after I moved out, Kate took up with him. She'd always had a thing for musicians, and Luke certainly aspired to be one. Fucking trumpet players. All he did was showboat and blast high notes. He thought his problem was chops. He'd been hanging around the clubs for years. "I've been sheddin', Tim," he told me whenever I saw him. "I've been sheddin' like crazy." There wasn't a leader who would hire him. The guys on the scene all considered him a little tweaked—desperate, basically pathetic. I guess Kate just needed to find the very bottom.

Holly told me how it went when Kate finally ended it with him. He called all hours of the night, sent e-mail after e-mail, had big bouquets of red roses delivered, followed by white lilies, and then, for some reason, a series of cactuses. Kate felt bad about the whole thing, Holly said. But she got nervous whenever she thought she saw Luke's car parked on Halsted Street.

The next few boxes were full of textbooks and case studies. There were a few old LPs in there too, most of them mine, but I wasn't interested in taking back stuff I'd left behind. I dumped the contents of the last box on the floor and started sifting through it.

Suddenly I felt another presence in the room. Something nudged me from behind, in the small of my back, and for a moment I wondered how Luke could've come in so close without my noticing. I pictured him pressing his knee into my back, pushing me down to the floor. When I turned around, I saw that it was a cat.

It was a huge thing, brown and white striped—a loaf of marble rye with legs. A gargling emerged from its gut, more a drain clearing than a purr. It butted up against me again.

I'd seen the cat dish. It hadn't occurred to me to put a cat with it. Kate had always hated cats.

"Luke, get in here."

He came in with the mask still pulled down over his face. In his right hand, he held an aluminum softball bat. "You find some shit in people's closets," he said, squaring up and taking a few practice swings. I felt the air move against my cheek. The cat jumped away and buried itself under the couch so that only the tip of its tail showed. "I never knew she was a sportswoman."

"Put that thing down," I said. And then, "She isn't."

Luke's eyes followed the end of the bat as he swung again. "It's for intruders." He turned to me, pointed the bat at my stomach. "For bad men. For guys like us."

He was acting tough. In wet clothes, he wasn't more than a hundred forty pounds.

"Where'd the cat come from?" I said

"That's Lover."

"*Lover?*"

"She got him awhile back. Guess she likes another warm body around."

I don't know what fucked me up more—that Kate had a cat named Lover, or that Luke was still referring to her in the present tense.

"It needs something. Food, water, I don't know."

Luke let the bat dangle, leaned on it like a cane. "Shit, don't sweat it. Lardball probably won't even come out again."

"What's in the bedroom?"

"Chick stuff. Dresses, shoes, gossip magazines."

The gargling sound came from underneath the couch. "I'm going to feed that thing."

"Oh, he likes food. You should see him wolf down the Sheba."

I closed my eyes, took a few deep breaths, checked my watch. "It's four fifteen already."

"We got all weekend."

"No. In and out, that's what we talked about. I'll feed the cat, then we get back to it."

"Sure, Tim," Luke said softy, looking injured. "You're the leader on this one."

I went into that cavernous kitchen and poked around in the cabinets. I found a box of dry food and shook some into the cat dish. As soon as the food hit, Lover came bounding in. I watched his neck accordion as he swallowed it down. "Lover," I said out loud, trying that silly, girlish name. I reached down and stroked his back. He bristled but went on eating.

There were boxes on top of the microwave and the fridge and a balled-up newspaper on the counter. I started raking through one of the boxes but then gave up on it. I stood at the center of the four shadows of me cast by the overhead spot lighting and felt something awful creep over me. If Kate had a cat, then someone, Holly maybe, was coming over to feed it—someone else would be first to see that the apartment had been broken in to. I'd wanted to hurt Kate, wanted to picture the look on her face when she opened the door and saw her home had been violated. Now even that small revenge had been denied me.

I rested my hands on the cold marble counter. The apartment had been my home nearly three years. Now it felt like a catacomb, a morgue. I started pulling open drawers. Most were empty. I yanked open the drawer under the microwave.

There they were. Two tiny square boxes—one Tiffany blue, the other a furzed pea green.

At first it stung, to be cast away in a junk drawer. Then I saw what else was in there: ten, fifteen envelopes of photos, several more framed pictures, a hospital bracelet that had Kate's mom's name printed on it.

I took up the framed pictures. A shot of Kate graduating from law school, standing in her gown. Two pictures taken on a ski hill—Kate and her brothers when they were teenagers, smiling out of puffy coats, scarves, and hats. A view across the lake where her dad lived in Michigan, the setting sun on the waves. Black and whites of her grandparents and some older relations whose names I didn't remember.

And then a photo of Kate and me. I held it up to the light, held it as gingerly as an artifact. It was from our early days—Kate in a sundress, her blond hair curling over her shoulders, me with a buzz cut trying to look serious. I was looking straight into the camera, but Kate was turned to me with a shy smile on her face. My favorite picture of her. You could see she was in love.

We lived disjointed lives, but for a long time that didn't matter. Kate would leave the apartment at seven every morning, eager to make an impression at her new practice. At noon, I got up to teach my lessons, then went straight to a gig. I'd get home at two or three in the morning, wake her up, and we'd fuck till we burned each other up. Being with her was like a circuit connecting, and lighting everything up.

I opened the ring boxes. There they were. One a thin, shining titanium band with three round, brilliant diamonds. The other cheap, tarnished gold, a hazy little stone stuck to it like an afterthought. It was Luke's grandma's or great-aunt's wedding ring. He sprang it on Kate one night, probably after he sensed things were going south. "He told her she was the best thing that ever happened to him," Holly said, "and that he couldn't stand living without her." Then he unfurled the whole story about his grandma or aunt or whatever, a sad story, apparently. "You have to feel for the guy," Holly said. "He wouldn't hear no." But after all his calls and e-mails and special deliveries, she said, you couldn't blame Kate for not searching him out to give the ring back.

Me, I'd spent four months shopping for that Tiffany, had blown most of the cash I'd made touring with a god-awful radio-rock band on it. I planned everything — oysters, champagne, dancing. It was a month after Kate's mom died, and I thought I could move into that hole, fill up the void in her life. That night, she was drunk, her kisses tasting like brine from the oysters.

I closed the ring boxes and ran my thumb over the velvet tops. We were done. I could go home to my efficiency, crawl into bed, wake up free of the shitted-up world Luke had dragged me into. I could start to forget everything that had happened.

But Kate's smell was everywhere. I breathed it in, storing it up. Then I rearranged the photos, shut the drawer, and slipped the rings into my pocket.

In the living room, the bat lay on the carpet beside the couch. What kind of burglar went through your old bills, took a few practice cuts with your softball bat, and then fed your cat?

I went into the bedroom. Luke was lying on the bed, his shoes off, mask rolled up, a pillow clutched to his chest. When I came in, he pushed himself up on his elbows. He was sweating and his eyes were bright.

"What the fuck are you doing?"

"Testing the mattress." He punched the covers lightly. "Firm."

"Get back to work. We'll never find the rings like this."

He slid his legs over the side of the bed, pushed his shoes on, and moved past me into the living room. I could've reached out and throttled him. Instead I just stood staring at the rucked-up sheets, the imprint of his skinny body. All I could think: He was the last to have her. Of all the fucking idiots in the world, Kate chose *him*.

In the living room, he flopped down on the couch.

"I'm half-asleep," he said with a yawn. "It's getting too late for this shit."

"No, it's early." I went to the window and opened the curtains. Across the staggered rooftops of the city, the huge dark sky was beginning to gray. "It's early," I said again. "Time to rise and shine."

When Kate called off the engagement, I felt, I don't know, relief. In the first weeks after I proposed, it was almost like we'd started over again. Then we began to drift. We argued about who did the grocery shopping, the laundry, who paid the lion's share of the rent—she did, and I hated that, and hated that I was failing to fill up the hole in her life. I resented her making me feel irrelevant and powerless. When she called things off, I told her I'd move out. All I needed was a place to store my drums and sleep. I believed I was leaving with dignity.

In my pocket I ran my fingers over the ring boxes. Kate had tried to give the Tiffany back, though I told a few buddies otherwise. My father taught me to stick to principles, no matter how dumb: Once a thing was given, it couldn't be taken back.

Behind me, Luke let out a long sigh. On the couch, he had his knees drawn up to his chest. He knit his brow like he was concentrating hard. The first time I saw him at a club, sitting up front, staring at the bandstand, it was obvious how bad he wanted to be up there playing. That intensity, that longing—that must have been what Kate saw too. She must have needed that heat, to be wanted that badly. He wasn't necessarily a terrible-looking guy.

"The rings aren't here," Luke said. "I bet she pawned them." He shook his head in disbelief.

"We could search the closets. There's a shitload more boxes."

"You know *what*?" His voice rose, then broke. "That's fucking cold. How could she be that cold?" His eyes were rimmed red, and I saw that he'd been crying earlier and was doing everything he could not to cry now. Jesus, it was embarrassing.

"It's okay," I said. "It'll be okay."

He nodded, but the words had no effect on him. "A girl like Kate," he said, "she's out of my league, you know? You've got to work to satisfy a girl like that." He smiled ruefully. "I mean, sometimes it took her *forever* to get there."

"Yeah"—I could feel myself starting to shake—"sometimes you have to put in the time. Practice. It's all about practice, right?"

"You know what my problem is, Tim? My lips." He pursed them and made a brief, high-pitched buzz. "I just never had the lips for the instrument."

A can of paint sat on the bookshelf. There were paint cans everywhere. I drummed my fingers on the lid—habit, my eternal
habit—listened to the falling note it made. How can something
full sound so empty? In my pocket, I touched the corners of the
ring boxes.

When Kate and I broke up, we'd promised we'd keep in touch.
After I heard about her and Luke, I couldn't keep that promise. She
called me, and I was brusque. I made it clear she wasn't forgiven.

But two months later she kicked Luke to the curb. I thought I
could comfort her. I called her up. "I heard about your trouble," I
said. "Holly told me. You doing okay?"

"How's Holly?" Kate said.

"You tell me"—I'd sought Holly out, but I wasn't going to tell
Kate that—"she's your friend."

"I'm glad you two still talk. She's fond of you."

"I'm playing right around the corner next Friday," I said. "At
this joint on Clark. Why don't you come down and check it out?"

"What kind of music?" she asked. I was always playing with
some new band.

"Straight-ahead stuff. You'd like it. Come on down. I'll buy you
a drink. We'll catch up."

Kate didn't speak for a long moment. It was like waiting for the
judge to read your sentence.

"It's just . . . Tim, I just don't think I'm ready right now."

"Ready for what? Come on, one drink. I need to see you."

"I can't. . . . Tim, I'm really sorry, but—"

I cut her off. "Why'd you give up on us? Didn't you even *want*
to give it a second chance? I mean, Christ, you didn't wait long to
start going with that fuck-nut Luke."

"Tim, please, I can't just go back to the way things were. I can't
just repeat things."

"What the fuck does that mean?"

She started to say something about circumstances, about it not
being my fault, it was something deeper than that, something
outside our control. Sometimes love just died and you couldn't do
anything about it. You couldn't even say why. Maybe if her mom
hadn't gotten sick. Maybe if we hadn't both been so focused on
our careers . . .

I didn't want to hear it. I pressed the receiver to my lips and let loose with all the rage and regret I'd been holding back. The things I said—I was out of my head. On the other end, every-thing went quiet. "Kate?" She hadn't hung up, but she must have put down the phone. In the background I heard a sound I thought was her sobbing, but I wasn't sure. "Kate, come on now, I didn't mean it. It's just, this is all fucked up, everything is fucked up." I waited. "Are you there? Come on, I love you, can't you see? Come on, answer me already." Nothing.

The sun was knifing into the living room. It was daylight. Luke sat in a trance, staring up at the bright scrim of dust motes hang-ing in the air. "Fuck," he said. "It's morning already. We got to finish what we started." He rose from the couch and started pac-ing. He took up the bat, trailing it behind him, leaving tracks in the carpet. With his free hand, he kept picking things up, tossing them aside, still searching. He picked up a copy of *Sense and Sen-sibility* from the coffee table. Kate read it several times a year. Ev-ery few months, that paperback with its frilly-costumed cover re-appeared. Luke flipped a few pages, then threw it away and picked up a Florida coffee mug with a cartoon sun wearing sunglasses. I'd bought it for her as a gag down in the Keys two years back, when we went deep-sea fishing with Eldridge. Luke dropped it on the coffee table, and the handle broke off. He was getting worked up. He took a CD from the top of the stereo. Dolly Parton. He threw the disc on the carpet and ground it under his heel.

"Here," I said, holding out his ring box on my open palm, "this is yours."

The bat fell to the carpet with a thud. He opened the box, took the tarnished ring out of its velvet cozy, and slid it onto his little finger. The stone flashed in the light.

"You know what we did?" he said, staring at the ring, as if addressing it. "We talked about you. Man, I hated it. I fucking hated it. But that's what the rebound guy does, right? Listen to her bitch about her ex. By the end of the night, she'd be crying on my shoulder. Sometimes I think the only thing we had in common was that we both knew you. And I don't even know you that well. But I thought, if I just put up with it long enough . . ."

The room was full of light. He blinked away a tear.

"She didn't think you were such a bad guy," I said.

"Yes, I am. Pathetic. Fucking pathetic." He sank to the floor, till he was cross-legged with the bat in front of him. It was time for us to get out. Half an hour maybe, and we could put the apartment back in some kind of order. Kate wouldn't have to find it like this.

"She liked how intense you were," I said. "You made her feel special."

He sat there, rolling the bat back and forth on the carpet. I tried to think of something else to reassure him. Just then a flutter of bird wings made me look at the window. A pigeon cooed outside. Lover poked his head out from under the couch.

He stalked across the carpet, taking small careful steps, waddling. When he got close to the window, he took a leap and batted the glass. The pigeon flew off, and Lover sat on his hind legs, confused, the corners of his mouth turned up as if in a smile.

"Here, kitty, kitty," Luke said, scratching at the carpet with his finger, beckoning.

Lover went to him and rubbed up against his leg. Luke ran his hand down Lover's back, but that wasn't what Lover wanted. He butted Luke's thigh.

"Cut it out, Lardball," Luke said. "Fucking cat." He pushed Lover away, and Lover bared his teeth. Luke picked up the bat and took a clumsy swing. The cat jumped away, and as the bat came around it knocked over a can of paint. The lid came open, and blue paint spread across the carpet.

He looked at me then, his eyes asking me to pull him back.

"Make it quick," I whispered.

He started with the one can, but that didn't satisfy him. With a couple blows from the bat, the cans came open easily enough. Swinging them, Luke threw bright bands of color—baby blue, beige, sunflower yellow—across the walls and furniture. He grinned and swung another can across the room. Paint spattered my shoes and my pants, but I didn't care. I just kept watching, frozen by the thrill of it.